ONE
HUNDRED
FLOWERS

ONE HUNDRED FLOWERS

Genki Kawamura
Translated by Cathy Hirano

ITHAKA

First published in the UK by Ithaka Press
An imprint of Bonnier Books UK
5th Floor, HYLO, 103–105 Bunhill Row,
London, EC1Y 8LZ

Owned by Bonnier Books
Sveavägen 56, Stockholm, Sweden

Paperback – 978-1-80418-959-7
Ebook – 978-1-80418-960-3
Audiobook – 978-1-80418-961-0

A CIP catalogue of this book is available from the British Library.

Typeset by IDSUK (Data Connection) Ltd
Printed and bound by Clays Ltd, Elcograf S.p.A

3 5 7 9 10 8 6 4 2

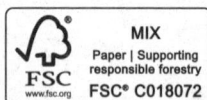

FSC
MIX
Paper | Supporting
responsible forestry
www.fsc.org   FSC® C018072

Every reasonable effort has been made to trace copyright holders of material reproduced in this book, but if any have been inadvertently overlooked the publishers would be glad to hear from them.

www.bonnierbooks.co.uk

For my grandmother,
who inspired this book at the close of her life
when her memories bloomed like a hundred flowers

1

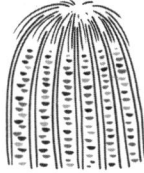

I open the front door to a wide yellow sky.

Not a cloud to be seen, but no sun either. Head down the hill, turn left at the corner. Better hurry. Izumi will be here soon. Houses, similar in shape, line the gently sloped street. The sound of a piano drifts from a house somewhere. Schumann's 'Träumerei'. The pianist keeps getting stuck at the second bar. Wait – I have to teach piano today. Miku, pay attention to those notes – do and fa. Oh dear, it's almost time for our lesson. But I have to go somewhere first. Where? Where am I going? Oh right, the supermarket in front of the station. Izumi's coming tonight. I'll make hayashi rice and sweet rolled omelette. His favourites. With big tomato slices on the side. Is there still mayonnaise? I'll get some just in case. He'll be arriving at the station soon. Got to get the shopping out of the way first. Better walk faster.

The click-click of shoes against asphalt echoes down the empty street. A swing comes into view, its rusted chains swaying. Perhaps a child was playing on it a moment ago. A small park beside a set of steep steps. A well-worn slide, a see-saw, a set of swings. Soundlessly, a red commuter train rolls by at the foot of the steps. Apartment buildings, all jammed together in the social housing development, stretch down the far side of the tracks beneath a dandelion-coloured sky. The sea should lie beyond them, but it's shrouded in haze. *Yuriko, what're you going to do?* Turning, I see my father. *You'd better get a hold of yourself and think it through carefully*, my mother says. She dabs her eyes with a hankie. *Mum, Dad, I'm sorry. I can't leave this child.* My mouth moves but the words make no sound; just a hiss of dry air escapes my lips. *Well, if you insist, there's nothing we can do.* My father averts his eyes, turns away. My mother follows. I want to run after them, but my legs won't move. What should I do? Somebody help! My mother and father disappear from sight, and I sink onto the swing, swaying from its rusted chains, and stare at the yellow sky. With a brittle sound like a crack snaking through glass, the sky splits open. A smooth, blank whiteness appears in the breach just as the ground heaves in undulating waves. Buildings in the housing estate fall like dominos in the distance. Izumi . . . The name bursts from my lips. *Izumi! Izumi!* I scream his name again and again. Oh . . . Izumi will be arriving at the station any minute now. But Asaba is waiting for me. I have to go. He's waiting. I have to buy onions and carrots and beef. Mayonnaise too. But I'll never make it in time. It's time for Miku's piano lesson. The second bar of 'Träumerei'. Pay attention to those notes – do and fa. Mum, Dad, I'm sorry. The white fissure in the sky darkens. Fireworks shoot into the greyish-yellow heavens – one burst, then another. A strange display. Only the top half is visible. As I watch the glowing semicircles rise, one after the other, my eyes fill with tears. Why are they so beautiful?

✽ ✽ ✽

Izumi Kasai arrived home to find his mother wasn't there.

Slipping off his shoes in the entranceway of the ageing house, he called out, 'Mum?' His voice echoed down the dark hallway. No light shone in the living room at the far end. There was no sign of life upstairs either, and the house was so chilled it felt colder than outside. He pulled up the zip of his down jacket. He had walked from the station, anticipating the warmth of home, but now he was shivering.

He headed towards the kitchen. A rank odour pricked his nostrils. The room where his mother should have been cooking dinner was empty. Turning on the light, he saw a pile of dirty dishes in the smallish sink. A pot with the remnants of cooked Chinese cabbage sat on a burner. This seemed odd for his meticulous mother. She had always kept up with the dishwashing.

As a boy, the only time he had ever washed the dishes was when she was too sick to get out of bed. He would come home from school, grab a chair and pull it to the sink, then fill the sponge with suds, standing on tiptoe to reach. When he proudly reported all this to his mother, as if it were some great feat, she would raise herself up in bed to say, 'Thank you, Izumi. You're amazing!'

One time he'd been so pleased with himself that he washed the dishes the next morning too. He felt his hand slip, but by then it was too late. The bowl was one his mother had treasured ever since she'd bought it in Kyushu over a decade before, when she was young. Alarmed by the sound, his mother rushed into the kitchen and, catching sight of the bowl broken neatly in two, grasped Izumi's hand in hers. 'Are you all right?' she asked. 'Did you cut yourself?' A drop of blood welled up on his index finger as if a ladybird had landed there. Izumi gasped, and his mother popped his finger in her mouth. Warm saliva coated his fingertip, and he was overcome with remorse.

In quick succession, Izumi turned on the light, the heating unit and the TV in the living room, which extended without a partition from the kitchen. A well-used grand piano occupied the room's centre. The TV, modest in size, stood beside it, along with a stereo.

The piano had always been at the centre of his mother's life. After graduating from a private music college, she had made a living by performing at hotel lounges and other venues while also doing small solo concerts. She started teaching piano after Izumi was born to ensure a steady income.

Her reputation as an attractive and competent teacher spread rapidly through the neighbourhood, and she soon had many students. She'd taught Izumi, too, but she was so strict when teaching that she seemed like a different person. He found her quite scary. At the beginning of elementary school, aged six, he'd told her he wanted to quit, and she had looked at him a little mournfully. You should just play and not worry about what I'm teaching you, she told him. But she didn't reproach him. Music, she said, shouldn't be forced on anyone.

The grimy-looking heating unit groaned as it belched out lukewarm air. It smelled a little musty. Izumi rang his mother's mobile, but it went to voicemail after six or seven rings.

A framed snapshot stood near the window. Izumi and his mother dressed in light summer yukata as they posed side by side at the entrance of a ryokan. Maybe two years ago. Or was it three? It might have been even more. A rare shot of just the two of them. They'd been served sashimi – giant Ise lobster – in their room, and his mother kept raving about how delicious it was and how wonderful it would be if they could come again. She was so insistent that Izumi finally snapped, 'All right. I get it,' and she looked a little sad.

Izumi sat at the dining table and stared blankly at the TV. Before he had realised it, almost an hour had passed since he'd arrived. A large apartment complex blocked off part of the purple sky above his mother's garden. As the lights flicked on in one room after another, Izumi noticed he was hungry. His mother still hadn't come home. Even though he'd told her what time he was coming. It was getting dark outside, and there was no one in sight.

He went upstairs to his room and dropped his knapsack on the cheap pipe-frame bed he'd used since high school. It creaked. He glanced at the bookcase, its shelves lined with a few manga series and some alternative rock CDs. An old electric guitar stood beside it gathering dust. A dark-brown Telecaster his mother had bought him when he was going into junior high. He'd played in a band until his last year of university but had never mastered the guitar to his satisfaction.

He climbed down the steep wooden staircase, stooping to avoid hitting his head on the ceiling. His eyes fell on his mother's scarf where it lay thrown over the sofa in the living room. With a twinge of foreboding, he passed straight through to the front door. Shoving his toes into his canvas trainers, he stepped outside.

He walked down the gentle hill and turned left at the dead end. Where could she have gone? Without thinking, he broke into a jog. It was just what he needed to shake off the cold. His breath shone white under the street lamps. The year's end was rapidly approaching, and the streetscape was brighter than usual. The frosted-glass windows of the houses lining the hill glowed a milky white, and the sounds of televisions seeped into the street.

He turned down an alley, heading for the steep steps that served as a shortcut to the station. As he put his hand on the railing, he noticed a swing swaying in the park beside the steps.

There, beneath the feeble glow of a street lamp, was Yuriko.

She was gazing at the city lights spreading into the distance while the swing creaked back and forth. He approached quietly so as not to startle her. Wrinkles creased her softly lit profile, reminding him that she was ageing inexorably, yet her face had a girlish innocence. Though he was now quite close, she didn't see him, her eyes fixed on the lights below. She was smiling as though lost in some beautiful dream.

'Mum, what're you doing here?' Izumi gasped. He was still out of breath.

'Time . . . to go home,' Yuriko murmured as if to herself. 'Huh?'

'I should go home now.'

'Mum, what's going on?'

Finally, she turned to look at him. 'Oh. Sorry . . . Izumi.' Her eyes, wet and luminous, unnerved him. He'd never seen such an expression on her face before.

'You scared me,' he said. 'Because you weren't home.'

'I'm sorry. I got tired out shopping at the supermarket.'

Izumi noticed she had no shopping bags with her. 'You'll catch cold if you stay out like this,' he said. He walked over to the swing, took off his down jacket and placed it around her shoulders. She was wearing just a thin blue cardigan over a neatly ironed white blouse. Far too little for this time of year.

'What do you want to do, Mum? Shall we go home and have a hot cup of tea?'

'I need to buy some onions and carrots. And some beef too . . .'

'Why don't we go together then? To the supermarket in front of the station?'

Yuriko nodded emphatically, like a child, then turned her eyes back to the city below. A red train passed along the tracks that extended left to right. No passengers rode it, perhaps because it was New Year's Eve, and it cut across their field of vision at an oddly slow speed.

The supermarket in front of the station was like a mini amusement park. Four years earlier, a major chain had launched itself into the shopping district, which until then had consisted solely of small, privately owned shops. It was much too grand even for the term 'supermarket'. It sold everything from groceries to pharmaceuticals, household goods, appliances and clothing, but words like department store or shopping centre didn't seem to fit, and Yuriko always referred to it as the 'supermarket in front of the station'.

In a few hours, it would be New Year, and the food section was deserted. His mother walked a little faster than usual. 'Wait,' Izumi called out, hurrying after her with the trolley. Glancing at the shelves, he noticed they were lined with things like seasonings made with malted rice, antibody-boosting yogurt, and products claiming to be gluten-free or super foods. Things had changed considerably since his last visit.

There were no proper supermarkets in the central Tokyo neighbourhood where Izumi lived, so he usually ordered food and other necessities online and had them delivered. The algorithms on these retail sites were so advanced that they selected things he had bought before, things he was likely to buy next, and new items he might be interested in buying, and displayed them on the recommended items page. All he had to do was click on the recommendations and his shopping was done in no time.

Yuriko hurried from one aisle to another, muttering to herself, 'I'll need this too. Oh, and I'd better get that,' as she put tomatoes and carrots into the crimson shopping basket. Izumi worried that she was buying far more of each item than she needed.

When she chose the most expensive sausages and put them in the basket, Izumi pointed out a cheaper brand. 'Wouldn't this be better?' he asked. But she laughed and told him that when he was young, he'd cry if she didn't get the other kind. 'Was I really that selfish? I don't remember that at all,' he said.

'You've always been that way. So forgetful,' Yuriko said, reaching for a package of thinly sliced beef. 'I'll make hayashi rice and rolled omelette. Today, I'm going to make only your favourite things.'

She placed the brimming basket on the checkout counter, and Izumi held out his credit card for the cashier. His mother, however, stopped him and took her wallet from her pocket.

It was a designer leather wallet that Izumi had bought for her at a duty-free shop overseas, but now it bulged in the middle like a dorayaki pancake sandwich stuffed with sweet bean paste. When she opened it, the space for banknotes was jammed with receipts. His mother had always reorganised the contents of her wallet as soon as she got home, but today even the change compartment was bursting with coins. Izumi could not tear his gaze away from it. Yuriko hastily explained that she couldn't seem to do the maths in her head these days, so she just handed notes to the cashier and ended up with lots of change. Averting her eyes, as if embarrassed, she closed the wallet.

'Do you mind if I go up to the fifth floor?' Izumi asked after filling a shopping bag with vegetables. The ungainly looking bag started to tilt, and he reached out to steady it.

'Do you need something?' The bag Yuriko had filled looked round and symmetrical, all the items neatly arranged inside.

'Your house is cold, so I was thinking of buying some thermal undershirts.'

'I'm so sorry. The heating unit's been acting up lately.'

'It's not your fault. I'm just sensitive to cold, that's all.'

'That's right. You never liked cold weather.'

'Guess not,' he said, and laughed suddenly. He'd never liked hot weather either. As a boy, he had once told his mother, 'Cool and warm, that's the kind of weather I like,' and she'd rolled her eyes at him.

'Should I get you some too, Mum?'

'No, don't worry about me. I've got some other shopping to do.'

Izumi rode the escalator up four floors and searched for thermal wear. As he walked through the neatly organised store, he realised he was feeling relieved. He'd been with his mother less than an hour and already he felt suffocated. Even when they were just walking together silently, he felt somehow ill at ease.

Fifteen years had passed since he'd got a job and moved out. Although he lived only an hour and a half away, the frequency of his visits had gradually decreased; now, he came back about twice a year. He couldn't bring himself to leave her on her own at New Year, so it was their custom to celebrate the holiday together, but the last few years their conversation had flagged, and he spent most of the time just nodding while she talked. He was at a loss for how he should spend his time with her. When he was little, he'd done all the talking, but things had become reversed – ever since that year.

He picked up a thermal base layer marked 'extra warm' in bold characters. As he was checking the size and colour, he caught sight of the women's thermal wear on the neighbouring shelf. Although he felt strangely embarrassed to be buying matching underwear for his mother, he selected two women's thermal vests as well and headed for the checkout counter.

Coming down the escalator, he saw his mother at the entrance to the supermarket holding a white amaryllis. He was struck by her small oval face and the fairness of her skin. She seemed to have slipped back in time to the way he remembered her from his childhood. He recalled how proud he had felt at school entrance ceremonies and other events when his teachers or classmates would tell him, 'Izumi, your mum's so pretty.'

'Sorry, Mum. Did I keep you waiting?' She shook her head without answering and smiled gently above the single flower in her hand.

As they entered the house, Yuriko apologised for the mess and began clearing away the post scattered about the living room. Izumi told her not to worry and unwrapped the flower. A withered anemone was stuck in the vase on the table. Several shrivelled brown petals lay on the tabletop. His mother had always made sure there was a fresh flower in the vase. He removed the anemone and dumped the murky yellow water down the sink, then refilled the vase. When he slipped the amaryllis into the translucent water, the room seemed to brighten.

Yuriko began folding the laundry she'd brought in off the line. Izumi went into the kitchen and started putting the food from the shopping bags into the fridge. Inside, it was crammed with bits of leftovers in plastic wrap. The vegetable compartment held some limp spinach and carrots and one blackened banana. Two loaves of bread sat beside the rice cooker, neither of which appeared to have been touched. Drawing out a new loaf from one of the shopping bags, Izumi called out to his mother in the living room, 'Mum, you've bought too much bread.'

He pointed to the three loaves lined up by the rice cooker.

'I keep doing that recently.' She smiled sheepishly as she placed another bath towel on the pile, each folded neatly into a square.

'You were always like that, Mum.'

'I guess you're right. It's nothing new, is it?'

Many times, he'd watched her put more of the same kind of yogurt or ham into the fridge saying that these were the ones he liked, clinching her argument with 'and it was a bargain too'.

Yuriko took Izumi's place in the kitchen and donned an apron. She washed the rice at the sink, then started working simultaneously on the rolled omelette and the stew for the hayashi rice, deftly using the little stove. After putting the stew on one of the two burners to simmer, she washed the lettuce and sliced the tomatoes.

His busy mother, who used to teach piano during the day and work part-time at night, was an incredibly efficient cook. She seemed to produce several different dishes within minutes of entering the kitchen. When Izumi began living on his own, he'd tried doing this himself, but no matter what he did, he never figured out how to make multiple dishes concurrently. He remembered thinking at the time that it was like magic.

'Can I help?' he asked, but Yuriko, without bothering to look up from the cutting board, told him to go and watch TV or something. Savouring the aroma of the demi-glace, he stretched out on the sofa and watched the New Year's Eve singing contest, *Kōhaku Uta Gassen*. Dating back to the 1950s, it pitched popular male and female singers against one another, splitting them into the red and the white teams. An idol group with matching red hats cheered on a female *enka* singer with a phenomenally high voice. She was smiling in a way that made it hard to tell if she was pleased or annoyed by the support.

How many times had he watched this programme with his mother? They'd moved to this house when he was fourteen, so by now it must have been more than twenty times. How many more times would they watch it together? Ten? Twenty? More than thirty might be pushing it. He was suddenly aware that they'd already long passed the halfway point in their relationship as mother and child.

'The red team has the best lineup ever,' announced one of the MCs, the star of the NHK's current morning drama. She kept driving this point home in a bright voice, as if trying to remind everyone that tonight's programme was a contest between the men's red team and the women's white team – something the audience appeared to have completely forgotten.

'That's what actresses are like backstage, you know.' Izumi recalled the smug look on his boss's face as he'd said this. Izumi had met the actress at work once. She'd played a role in a music video for one of the label's artists whose piece had been chosen as the theme song for a movie. Being in charge of promotion, Izumi was present for the shoot. The actress barely uttered a word, even when selecting costumes or during filming – just the bare minimum required in greeting or response, plus the few lines for her part. There was no proactive involvement in the conversation whatsoever. On TV she came across as cheerful and vivacious, so her behaviour perplexed Izumi and the rest of the team from the record label. She was young, and at the time, Izumi had felt sorry for her: she'd been thrust into the unfamiliar music world too soon. But watching her on TV now, her voice strong and clear, he wondered if she'd just been enjoying the act. Perhaps for her, the girl laughing animatedly on the screen and the reticent girl who kept her head down that day were no more than roles in an entertaining play.

He heard his mother say, 'Dinner's ready.'

The table was heavy with his mother's cooking. Steam rose from a plate of hayashi rice, a gleaming mound of white rice half buried in tender beef sauce. Chunks of white turnip floated in a consommé soup. And there was fresh tomato and lettuce salad, sweet rolled omelette, dark-purple eggplant – deep-fried and marinated – and dried daikon strips stewed with sliced carrot. There were even traditional dishes essential for bringing in the New Year, like *namasu* – a marinated daikon and carrot salad – and stewed herring.

'Just as I thought. It's magic,' said Izumi as he took a seat at the table.

Yuriko was laying out the chopsticks. 'What is?' she asked.

'This. How did you manage to make it all so quickly?'

'Is it too much?'

'No, it looks great.'

'But I cheated a bit this year. The herring and the dried daikon are readymade. Sorry.'

'No need to apologise.'

'I'd like to make it all from scratch but—'

'Don't worry about it, Mum.'

'Sorry.'

'Mum, like I said—'

'You're right. Let's eat.'

'*Itadakimasu*,' they said in unison. The judges on TV were being asked for their opinion on the show so far. The exultant voice of the announcer rang through the living room. The TV had always been turned off during meals when Izumi was a boy, but on New Year's Eve, the rule was that they could watch while eating.

The onions in the stew were sweet, and the carrots tender without being too soft. The flavours mingled perfectly with the russet-coloured sauce. Izumi scooped up a spoonful of rice and stew and popped it in his mouth. His tongue was greeted by a faint tang, followed by the sweetness of demi-glace sauce. Unable to stop, he devoured one spoonful after another, huffing and puffing to cool each one down. His mother's hayashi rice was the best. Memories of peering into the kitchen, unable to wait for dinner, came flooding back.

Before Izumi knew it, all that was left on his plate was a bit of rice. 'Would you like some more?' Yuriko asked, and he nodded wordlessly. She took his plate and headed for the kitchen. The TV programme was gearing up for the finale, and a boys' band was singing and dancing while flashy images were projected onto the stage. Cheers which sounded more like screams rose from the audience. The MC announced that the performance incorporated the latest video projection technology, without explaining what made it the 'latest'.

Around the time they finished eating, the scene had switched to a snow-covered temple. The announcer proclaimed there were just a few minutes to midnight. Wondering what was on the other channels, Izumi pressed the remote. The faces of newscasters and athletes were sandwiched between a programme showcasing up-and-coming comedians and another featuring J-pop boy bands. Somehow all the other programmes seemed too loud, and he switched back to the original channel. 'All we need to know is when the new year starts, right?' said Yuriko, as if reading his thoughts.

The gong of temple bells on the TV ushered in the new year.

Bowing to Izumi, Yuriko wished him a happy new year using the honorific form of speech. Izumi bowed and replied in kind. It was the one moment in the entire year when they spoke to each other in formal, rather than casual, Japanese. Izumi smiled self-consciously, and Yuriko smiled back.

His phone began to buzz with New Year's greetings from friends and co-workers. He sent a brief message to Kaori, who had gone to her parents' home for New Year's, and she replied right away. 'Happy New Year. Be good to your Mum.'

'How's Kaori?' Yuriko asked, right on cue, as if she'd seen the message.

'Fine. She said to say Hi,' he replied, keeping his eyes on his phone.

'I see. It's been a long time.'

'How old are you, Mum?' Izumi asked, trying to divert her attention. He nibbled on a piece of stewed herring that remained on a plate.

'Don't ask,' she said. 'I don't want to count.' She shook her head as she started piling up the empty dishes.

'But today's the day, right?'

'When you get this old, it doesn't matter anymore.'

'Sixty-nine?'

'Sixty-eight.'

'Oh. Sorry.'

'I'm used to it. You do that every time.'

With an apologetic smile, Izumi fixed his eyes on his mother's face. He waited for her gaze to shift from the plates on the table to him, then said, 'Happy Birthday, Mum.'

His mother was born on New Year's Day. Every year, they greeted the New Year together and then celebrated her birthday, just the two of them.

'No one forgets my birthday, but they always forget me.'

Everyone remembered that she was born on New Year's Day, but when that day came, they all forgot to wish her happy birthday. Busy with their families, no one was ever free to celebrate it with her, and all the restaurants were closed. She ate traditional New Year's dishes instead of cake, and sometimes her birthday present ended up being a charm picked up while visiting a shrine. If anyone asked her when she was born, Yuriko always expressed regret that it was on New Year's Day, concluding with a laugh, 'Happy Birthday just can't compete with Happy New Year.'

Her one solace was a childhood friend who'd been born on the same day. Sharing this birthday made them feel they were destined to be friends.

Izumi's mother told him about this friend when he was eleven. It was the first time he'd ever bought his mother a birthday present. On New Year's Eve, he wandered through the shopping arcade wondering what to get her, and finally settled on a single narcissus flower. It was the only flower left in the shop before closing. Taking the slender package from his hands, she had thanked him, her voice almost like a sigh, and hurried from the living room. She didn't return for some time.

Izumi waited uneasily, filled with regret. Maybe a flower had been the wrong choice. Should he have bought her some cream puffs, which he knew she liked, instead? His mother returned, red-eyed. 'Why did you pick a white flower?' she asked. 'The colour I love best?'

'It was the only one left,' Izumi said truthfully, then added, 'I don't think I could have decided by myself if there'd been more.'

'I'm so glad today is my birthday,' murmured his mother, her voice once again like a sigh. Then she picked up a photo from among those lined up along the window, one from when she was in high school, and began telling him about her childhood friend.

Yuriko and her friend used to exchange presents and have their own birthday party, just the two of them, on New Year's Day. They went to the shrine and from there to a movie. It made them feel special, like chosen ones. They read their horoscopes and assumed they were destined to share all the joys and sorrows to come.

But in the spring of their seventeenth year, Yuriko's friend was killed in a traffic accident. More than sorrow, Yuriko felt dazed and disorientated. Even the funeral seemed unreal. To lose the one person who'd lived life at exactly the same time she did felt like losing a part of herself. She would never again believe in horoscopes, whether in magazines or on TV.

'I thought we shared the same fate, so when she died, my birthday lost any meaning. But if I can celebrate it with you, then the meaning will change.' She smiled and said, 'Thank you, Izumi,' as she placed the white narcissus in a clear glass.

From then on, every year Izumi gave his mother a present on New Year's Day. A handkerchief, a teacup, a pouch, a pendant. And from the day he had given her the first one, Yuriko had always kept a single flower in a vase. Always, without fail, like some kind of promise between the two of them. Except for that year.

'But even so . . .'

At the sound of his mother's voice, Izumi's focus zeroed in on a blur of silver. He was on his sixth can of beer, and one of the empty cans lay in front of his eyes like a gleaming insect. 'What?'

'Just the usual.'

'What is?'

'No messages.' Yuriko shook the smartphone she had bought last autumn. At the time, she'd emailed him repeatedly saying she couldn't figure out how it worked.

'You'll get birthday wishes in the morning,' he said. He shifted his gaze to her face.

'I guess so. I hope people haven't forgotten.' She smiled, her eyes moist again. She exuded the radiance of a young woman in love. Where that came from, Izumi had no way of knowing.

2

It looked like a cloud passing across the night sky.

'About six centimetres. The size of a kiwi fruit.' The doctor kept his eyes on the monitor while running the ultrasound probe over the slight bulge in Kaori's abdomen. Izumi watched the device sliding over the curve of her skin. The cloud swirling on the screen took on human form.

'A kiwi?' Lying on the examination table, Kaori moved her index finger away from her thumb as if measuring six centimetres. Izumi shifted his gaze to her fingertips. The walls of the room were spotlessly white and smelled faintly of disinfectant. The only thing imparting colour to the room was a picture of rapeseed flowers on the calendar.

'Hmmm, a bit smaller than that. Maybe about the size of a strawberry.'

'A strawberry.' Kaori shortened the gap between her fingers. 'Either way, the comparison is still a fruit.'

'You're right. I can't think of anything else. Can you?'

'A macaroon? Or a cream puff?'

'A little too sweet I think,' laughed the obstetrician. His plump figure reminded Izumi of a cook rather than a doctor.

Kaori laughed too. 'That's true. It makes me think I'll gain weight,' she said. 'How about a tennis ball or a ping-pong ball?'

'That's a brilliant idea. I'll give it a try,' the doctor exclaimed, raising his index finger with a delighted expression. His white coat was too big; when he put his arm down, the sleeve covered his hand all the way to his fingertips.

Izumi had listened wordlessly to their exchange, but now he asked, 'How's the baby? Is everything okay?'

'Oh, sorry. Of course, you feel a bit anxious, don't you?' The doctor pointed to the screen. 'Look there. The heart's beating strongly. Your little ping-pong ball is doing fine.'

'That's a relief,' said Izumi, his voice hoarse. He glanced at Kaori. From where she lay, she mouthed, 'Great,' and squeezed his hand.

The human-shaped cloud moved slowly. The tiny heart in the centre pulsated as though blinking. He still couldn't believe there was a life in there. Or that he would soon be a father.

'You must be excited. In half a year, you'll be a mum and dad.' The obstetrician gave them a friendly smile as he wiped the gel from the device, signalling that their appointment was over.

Izumi thanked him and rose to open the white door. As he did so, he thought he heard someone call him, and turned to look. His eyes fell on the ultrasound monitor. But the night sky and swirling cloud were gone, leaving only darkness.

'You don't need to come every time, you know. You have work to do,' Kaori said after they'd left the hospital and hopped on a train at the nearest station. The afternoon Sobu line was relatively empty, and they sat side by side.

'Really? Don't most fathers go?' he asked, taken by surprise. He glanced at her profile. Her eyes were fixed on the cherry trees outside the window. They'd be thick with pink blossoms come spring, but were just grey bark and branches now.

'Jun said her husband never went, not even once.'

'That's bad.'

'But pretty common. A lot of guys feel uncomfortable in a maternity ward.'

'Oh.'

'I can kind of understand. I mean, they keep you waiting a long time. Sometimes half a day, even when you've got morning sickness.'

Kaori gripped the sides of her dark blue leather handbag. She always did that when the nausea was bad. 'Are you okay?' Izumi asked. Insisting that she was fine, she drew a carton of apple juice from her bag, inserted the straw, and drank it in one go. It was her 'morning-sickness stopper' that she carried with her everywhere. There was no maternity tag hanging from her purse yet. She'd received one from the municipal office but was reluctant to use it. When Izumi had asked why she didn't display the tag, she'd told him it made her feel somehow embarrassed to expect commuters to give up their seat for her.

'But this only happens once or maybe twice in a life-time,' Izumi said.

The train picked up speed and passed along the edge of an urban fishing hole, a section of river partitioned into rectangular pools stocked with fish. Even though it was mid-afternoon on a weekday, the place was packed with people. They all sat on upturned plastic beer crates, their fishing lines dangling in the water. From a distance, it didn't look like they were catching any fish.

'Izumi, I'm worried you might be overdoing it. If you push yourself, you won't be able to keep it up,' said Kaori, flattening and then folding the empty juice carton. It was her habit when discarding paper things. Lunch wrappers, used table napkins, chopstick sleeves. Anything like that she folded up into a compact square.

'I'm not overdoing it,' said Izumi, as the train pulled into the station above the fishing spot.

Kaori stepped off and began walking down the narrow platform, which was sandwiched between two trains, one yellow and one orange. Aiming his voice at the back of her head, Izumi explained it was precisely because he didn't know anything about being a parent that he was open to trying everything.

Exiting the ticket gate, they crossed the road and began walking up a hill past various shops: a coffee chain, a book and record shop, a beef-bowl restaurant, a convenience store. A cold wind struck Izumi's face.

'It's surprising how clearly you can see it, isn't it?' he said, pulling up the collar of his wool coat.

'See what?' She glanced at him, adjusting the strap of her handbag on her shoulder. The incline grew steeper near the top. He reached out to take her bag, but she shook her head. She didn't like Izumi carrying things for her.

'The baby. In the ultrasound.'

'Oh, yeah. But apparently there's 3D ultrasound now.'

'Really? What's that?'

'The baby looks three-dimensional. I've heard the images are incredibly real. Recently, there's even 4D.'

'Four dimensional?'

'It's what they call it when the 3D images are constantly updated, so you can see the baby move as well.'

'Amazing.'

'Like a movie,' Kaori said, then laughed, adding, 'But I guess movies aren't exactly four dimensional.'

They reached the top of the hill and turned right. A huge grey building defined by square windows came into view. The sun hit the hilltop, warming the air a little.

'But it's so cute, I can see why people would want to get a better picture.'

'Are you serious?'

'Of course.'

'Doesn't it look like some kind of alien?'

'Don't say that,' Izumi chided her.

Kaori paused, then continued. 'You don't really expect me to see an ultrasound as cute, do you?'

'Guess not. You're always so pragmatic.'

'Maybe, but I bet a lot of people feel the same way. They just don't say so.'

'You think?'

They entered the grey building side by side. The door opened automatically, revealing two uniformed receptionists sitting at the front desk. They looked like identical twins. Both were focused on their laptops, raising their faces only when necessary to give a mechanical greeting. Izumi's co-workers often grumbled that robots could do a better job. A large screen beside the reception desk was playing a music video by a young hip-hop artist Izumi was currently in charge of. Despite the striking visuals, the lyrics made little impact. Even though it had seemed to have real potential when they finished it.

'When are you going to tell your mother?'

They walked through the lobby, casting the café space a quick glance as they passed, and got in the lift. Kaori pushed three and five, then turned to him.

'You're right,' said Izumi. 'I'd better tell her. You'll be in your second trimester soon.'

'As for me, I wonder how long I should . . .'

'Should what?'

'Work. I'd like to work until as close to the due date as possible. Even if I take time off, I'll have nothing to do.' She shrugged. She had already told her immediate boss and the personnel department she was pregnant.

'You should've heard what my co-workers told me the other day,' said Izumi.

'What?'

'That I should have the baby.'

'Why?'

'They said you're better at your job, so I should be the one to give birth and raise it.'

'That's awful,' she said, and peered into his face. 'Were you shocked?'

It was true she was an excellent director, respected and well liked. Many departments had sought her for their team, but now that her dream of transferring to the classical department had been granted, she was busy planning and recording albums and managing concerts for artists signed to the label.

'I was not amused. I should've known what I was signing up for when I married someone from the same company.'

'I'm counting on you, dear husband.' Kaori flashed him an impish smile, just as the lift stopped with a loud ping at the third floor. The door opened and several junior co-workers got on, greeting Kaori when they saw her. She gave a quick nod in return and hurried from the lift.

'Thank you for purchasing my talent.' This was the first thing KOE had said to Izumi when they met. 'Please market me as your product. Otherwise, there'll have been no point in coming out into the world.'

KOE was discovered on the internet. Although her self-produced videos showed only her lips, the lascivious visuals hinted at a hidden beauty, and each one she released surpassed a million views. Major record labels began taking an interest about a year after her internet debut.

After stiff competition among five different labels, she had chosen the one Izumi worked for, and Izumi, who had noted her talent early on, volunteered to handle promotion. Kaori, two years his junior, was called in as assistant director.

At their first meeting, KOE made constant demands. Please limit the number of people at future meetings because I get overwhelmed if I have to talk with more than three people at once. Please switch the meeting to a room without a window because I don't like direct sunlight. Please bring me water because caffeine messes up my metabolism.

The staff greeted each demand with the type of smile they would have used to placate a child and scurried about in response to her wishes.

Izumi knew alarm bells were clanging in everyone's minds – this one's trouble. Yet by the end of the meeting, she'd won them over. Bowing deeply, she thanked everyone with a child-like smile as tears fell from her eyes. 'I was so nervous,' she whispered in a soft, finely textured voice, brushing away her tears. Behind him, Izumi heard one of the label's new employees sniffling. Beside him, Kaori's eyes widened as if she'd just realised KOE's potential.

The scene reminded Izumi of something the director in charge of artist development had told him after discovering KOE. 'Her gift goes beyond merely creating something. She wins the hearts and draws out the talent of others.' KOE filled all the conditions needed to make it big.

After this first meeting with KOE, Izumi returned to his desk to find that she had sent him an email. She started off with a brief introduction saying she'd got his email address from his business card, then wrote about how much she had staked on the future of her music. In a postscript, she added that she felt an affinity with Izumi and asked him to share any comments he had about her music, both the good and the bad. Izumi's spirits rose. It was as if she had chosen him specially. From then on, every time she finished a song, he would pick out lyrics that had particularly touched him and send her an email with his comments.

With the entrance of this phenomenal new artist, songwriters inspired by her lyrics vied for the chance to put them to music. Izumi visited television and film producers, playing them a demo tape with scratch vocals by KOE. He also convinced his boss to let him produce a lavish set of PR handouts. Impressed by the high quality, several producers got in touch, as well as some directors who had been fans since KOE first emerged on the internet. Izumi secured tie-ins for both a movie and a TV anime series. Preparations for KOE's debut moved forward with an exceptionally large project team for a new artist.

But one week before recording, KOE vanished.

No matter how many times her manager called, there was no reply. No one knew her whereabouts. Frustrated and impatient, the entire project team searched for her. Izumi emailed her many times, but she never replied.

'I found KOE. She's in Shibuya. Can you come now?' The phone call from Kaori came at two in the morning, five days after KOE had disappeared. Izumi threw a jacket over his T-shirt, dashed outside, and hailed a cab. He only realised after he got in that his T-shirt had a stupid-looking anime character on it. He did up the buttons on his jacket. Whenever he met KOE, he'd been careful to wear something plain and navy-coloured because that's what she liked.

'KOE actually stayed in touch with me even after she disappeared,' said Kaori. She was waiting for him in the lobby of a luxurious hotel in Shibuya. 'I was hoping I could somehow make her come round, but she kept saying "Those people wouldn't understand, no matter what I might say."' Kaori explained that it would just upset the department head to bring him in at this stage, making it impossible to get anywhere, so she'd asked Izumi to come instead. 'And,' she added as they rode the lift to the top, 'KOE said she feels she can trust you more than the others.'

Izumi was hurt that KOE had only contacted Kaori. He felt foolish for having believed her postscript claiming an affinity with him.

'KOE doesn't have a father, you see,' Kaori muttered to the lavender-hued city as their cab sped along the expressway.

The roads at dawn were empty, and the taxi glided along unimpeded. 'Mmm,' was all that Izumi said. He failed to grasp her point. And after four hours of talking with KOE, he didn't have the energy to ask.

The words 'doesn't have a father' drifted soundlessly between them.

The incandescent night view of Shibuya from KOE's penthouse suite had seemed blindingly bright. In addition to a staggering sign-on bonus, she was also receiving a monthly sum known as 'training compensation'.

'I've forgotten music.' KOE sat on the huge sofa with her legs curled up like a cat. 'I can't seem to remember how I wrote lyrics, and I no longer know what I should feel when I sing.' She would quit, she said, repeating that she couldn't express something she'd forgotten how to feel.

Sitting beside a silent Izumi, Kaori calmly asked one question after another. Why did KOE think so? How did this happen? What did she want to do next?

'I've found someone I love more than music.' Still gazing at the excessive brilliance of the buildings below, she began talking about the photographer, an older man with whom she had fallen in love.

'It seems so strange that I could open up like that to someone I'd only just met. Or maybe that isn't the right expression. It was more like he wrenched my heart out of me.'

After their first photo shoot, KOE had waited for him outside the studio. Many people passed her by on that crowded Friday night. Her face had yet to be released to the public, and to those on the street, she was still nobody.

'What's he like?' asked Kaori.

'He never talks about himself.' KOE smiled as if remembering something. 'But he did say he was recently divorced and that he's fed up with the social scene in Tokyo.'

Izumi would have liked to speed things up, but felt now wasn't the time to butt in. It was painstaking work, like stacking building blocks. One mistake in the order and the whole thing would come tumbling down.

Kaori continued slowly feeding KOE questions, like someone trying to coax a cat out from under a porch. 'And then what did you do?'

'I invited him to my hotel. I still can't believe I have any sexual desire. I've always had an aversion to men. I used to find their lust repulsive.'

Izumi was surprised by how objectively he listened to her story. He'd had a hunch that sooner or later something like this would happen. It was that very risk that had made KOE so enticing.

Three days after meeting the photographer, KOE had moved into his suite. She broke off contact with her manager and shut herself away, abandoning all her recording and promotion commitments. But the photographer announced he was planning to move to Brooklyn the following month. It was already decided, before we ever met, he said. As the son of a well-known actor, he received generous backing.

'There's nothing else I want,' KOE whispered, still curled up on the sofa. 'I'm going to Brooklyn. He's enough for me.' There was no trace of the finely textured, scintillating voice Izumi remembered from their first meeting. As if a spell had been broken, its lustre was gone. Her composure conveyed her resolve.

To foray any deeper into her world would be difficult. Kaori said nothing, as if she had given up. Izumi pulled himself together and tried to convince KOE to at least finish the songs she was working on before going to the States. He wanted to prove there'd been some meaning in the emails they'd exchanged.

'I'm a different person. The songs I wrote over these last few months, they're no longer my words or my music. The only choice is to throw everything away.'

She rebuffed him with the softness of someone falling asleep. Already her eyes seemed sunk in a dream. Outside the window, the sky grew lighter, and a pale blue spread across it. The glittering lights of Shibuya, which had seemed to vie for brightness, were quickly fading.

The taxi pulled up in front of the grey building. When Izumi and Kaori alighted, a deafening chorus of birdsong rained down from the trees lining the boulevard. They ducked into the building, as though fleeing the noise, and found everyone involved in the project, right up to the label's executive VP, waiting for them.

KOE left for the States the following month.

Smoke rose from charcoal braziers in the restaurant as Izumi raised his mug of beer. Kaori clinked hers against his.

The restaurant, which was next door to their office, was so popular it was hard to get a reservation. But their co-workers avoided it because of the poor service and the fact it was too close to the company for comfort. This made it a convenient place for Izumi and Kaori to meet and talk.

'Turns out she was a Korean dancer,' said Kaori as she reached with her chopsticks for some bean sprout namul.

'Who?' Izumi asked, nibbling on kimchi.

'KOE's rival in Brooklyn.'

'Oh, you mean the one the cameraman had an affair with.'

KOE had returned to Japan after half a year away. Kaori had launched into production as if she'd known all along KOE would be back. Recording sessions were held daily in a studio in Nakameguro, and the album came out nine months later than originally planned.

After KOE's first live concert promoting the album's release, Izumi had invited Kaori out to this barbecue restaurant.

'I don't think you could even call it an affair. Guys like him never take relationships seriously. He just succeeded in getting his hooks into her, that's all.' Kaori took a swig from her already half-empty beer mug.

'Hooks?' Mirroring her movements, Izumi brought his own mug to his lips.

'He knew what KOE wanted him to say and do. There was no deep philosophy behind his actions, and no love either. I think he simply played the person she wanted him to be.'

'Some guys excel just at that and nothing else.'

Upon her return, KOE had told them the past half year was a complete blank. She couldn't remember why she'd done what she did or why she'd loved him. Tears flowed nonstop from her glazed eyes.

Kaori patted her back and gave her the occasional hug while pressing on with recording. 'I've forgotten how to love,' KOE confessed. 'All the lyrics I wrote since coming back are just quoting things he said to me in Brooklyn.'

'Now I know why we failed,' said Kaori.

A waiter placed a platter of thick slices of tongue along with a plate of lemon wedges on the table. Kaori picked up a lemon wedge. Narrowing her eyes, she squeezed the juice onto a small plate.

'*We* failed? Wasn't KOE the one with the problem?' Izumi placed two slices of beef tongue on the charcoal brazier without touching the lemon. Lemon juice robbed the meat of any other flavour, he thought.

'We could've done more.'

'Like what?'

KOE's work after she returned was lacklustre. The magic never returned to her voice. She was over an hour late for every recording session and took so many anti-depressants before the taping of a radio programme to promote her album that her speech was slurred. One by one, her sponsors backed out.

'I think artists need both a mother and a father.'

'A mother and a father?'

'A mother is someone who compassionately accepts everything, while a father is strict and keeps you on the straight path no matter what. One without the other won't work. You need both.'

'You mean our project team only had mothers?'

'I tried to be a father figure, but in the end, I couldn't protect her. And it didn't help that she had no real father.'

Feeling uncomfortable, Izumi glanced around the shop. There wasn't much beer left in his mug, and he thought about ordering another, but all the waiters were gathered in front of the till chatting and laughing.

Album sales had started off well but soon petered out. Ultimately, the only ones who bought it were fans from

KOE's internet days. After the encore at the end of her first ever live concert, KOE told the audience she intended to retire from music indefinitely.

This time, Kaori was the one who insisted KOE should continue music. Kaori's tenacity made her seem a different person from the one who'd held back from persuading KOE that night in the Shibuya hotel.

Watching Kaori place chunks of thick red meat on the brazier, Izumi recalled her face as she had gazed out the window of the taxi that night – Tokyo tower rising grey against the purple sky.

'Does not having a father make so much difference?'

'What?'

'You've said that before, Kaori. That KOE doesn't have a father.'

'I guess I did.'

'Do you mean if KOE had a father, this wouldn't have happened? She wouldn't have fallen for that guy and ended up throwing everything away?' He suspected he sounded belligerent, but he couldn't stop himself.

Kaori kept her eyes on the hot red coals and continued placing pieces of meat on the grill. 'Well, I don't think we can say there's no connection. Especially when the guy was old enough to be her father.'

'But isn't that a bit superficial? It sounds like you're saying kids can't become decent people if they have bad or absent parents.'

A stench of charred meat rose from the grill. Izumi grabbed a pair of tongs and roughly flipped the smoking chunks.

'But that's not what I'm saying. I just meant that it has an impact.'

It was too late. All the meat was charred.

'Actually, I don't have a father either.' Izumi pushed the smouldering meat off to one side. Fat still dripped from the black lumps. 'He wasn't there from the time I was born. I don't even know his name or what he looks like.'

Kaori watched the smoke rising from the grill. 'I'm sorry,' she said. 'I didn't mean to make you feel bad.'

'I know.'

Not just his father. Izumi had never met his mother's father either.

Due to a series of unfortunate circumstances, Yuriko had decided to give birth alone. 'I was always a good little daughter, diligent and obedient, so I think my father just couldn't forgive me.' He never came to see her in the hospital, and although her mother had come once, she and Yuriko drifted apart soon after the birth.

On the evening of Izumi's graduation from elementary school, he and his mother had celebrated together at a nearby chain restaurant that served affordable family fare. It was then that she told him how she'd come to raise him on her own. 'I was always stubborn, you see,' she concluded with a smile. 'And just so you know, I chose your name when I was in the hospital because, regardless of whether you were a boy or a girl, I wanted to greet your birth with a joy that overflowed like a spring.'

On every special occasion, Yuriko had shared a memory with him from her own past.

As if to fill the sudden silence, Kaori placed thin strips of marbled meat on the grill. Flames rose instantly, enveloping the meat in smoke. Over the sound of fat sizzling as it hit the coals, Kaori murmured, 'Of course, I don't think it's bad not to have parents. Children can't choose. And in KOE's case, the environment in which she was raised inspired the music she wrote.'

'She might still have written great lyrics even if she'd had both parents though.' Izumi downed the rest of his beer. Once again, his eyes wandered in search of the waiters. But this time there was no one in sight. He clicked his tongue. There'd been so many just a moment ago.

'I guess that's possible too. But clearly, it was because she was unfulfilled that she could write such compelling lyrics.' Staring at the flaming meat, Kaori continued. 'Parents have tremendous influence. I know the power of that curse. That's why I spent so long trying to figure out how to escape. Then, one day I realised that someone who serves as a parent doesn't have to be a blood relation. My parents never divorced, but they could hardly be called a married couple. They couldn't even act like proper parents. I started learning ballet when I was about four. It was my ballet teacher who taught me how to live right.

I realised this only after growing up, but ever since, I've never considered blood relations or family to be absolute. People who aren't related can often complement each other. If a person lacks a father, someone else should be able to take on that role, and that's what I wanted to do for KOE.'

She said this all in a rush, then grabbed two or three slices of meat that were starting to char and shoved them in her mouth.

Watching her jaw chewing vigorously, Izumi suddenly felt silly for being so angry.

'What's up? Why're you smiling, Izumi?' she asked.

He realised he was grinning. 'Nothing,' he said. Spreading more slices of meat on the brazier, he covered up by asking, 'Should we order some rice?'

Kaori regarded him with her big dark eyes for a moment, then laughed. 'Yes!' she exclaimed. 'Extra-large!'

3

Izumi woke at the sound of the front door closing. He sat up in bed. The white sheets were contoured like whipped cream. No warmth remained in the space beside him. He stretched gently and caught a glimpse of scattered books and CDs from the corner of his eye.

We'll be needing space for things like picture books, so clear off some shelves in the bookcase. That's what Kaori had said, and Izumi had begun sorting last night, but had made little progress because he kept reminiscing over each item he picked up. Now that he listened to music on his phone or computer, he no longer used his CD player. All the music in those CDs was already on the web. Although just worthless discs now, they were so intimately tied to memories of listening to music that he found it hard to let them go.

He padded along the dark-brown flooring of the corridor to the living room. The apartment block was designed for families, and the rooms were generally spacious, making the sofa and TV he'd brought from his previous apartment seem oddly small and out of context. When looking for somewhere to live, he and Kaori had spent a long time discussing their 'vision of the future' before choosing which place to buy.

The sky outside was overcast, and a north wind sporadically rattled the windows, but the room was warm. Kaori must have left the floor heating on for him. He could feel the warmth seep into the soles of his bare feet. Two months ago, she'd told him she was pregnant. Having been married two years, it was a natural outcome, yet he found it unexpectedly disconcerting when it happened. He still struggled to connect the fact they were having a child with the fact he would become a father.

Three empty chocolate bar wrappers, neatly folded, were stacked on the dining table. She must have started her day with chocolate again, he thought. Kaori's morning sickness had abated over the last few weeks. But she was now devouring tons of chocolate. 'Isn't that a bit much?' Izumi had said recently. 'I guess it's better than not eating anything at all, but still.' To drive his point home, he mentioned someone who'd gained too much weight during pregnancy and consequently had a hard time during labour 'because the baby gained weight too'.

'I know, but . . .' Kaori had said. She stroked her stomach with her left hand, as though drawing circles. In the other, she clutched a chocolate bar in a red wrapper. 'I can't stop myself. It's a craving that goes beyond hunger.'

'And the fact that chocolate is all you're eating. It just seems so unhealthy.'

'I remember people saying pregnant women crave sour things, like lemon or grapefruit.'

'That would be an improvement. At least you'd be getting some vitamin C.'

'Yeah, but none of the women I know get healthy cravings. All my friends want things like French fries, Coke or ice cream.'

'Really? Those all sound so bad for you.'

'I know. I wonder why we want to eat things we normally have no interest in when there's a baby inside us.' Kaori sank her teeth into the chocolate bar. Her round bite mark ignored the neatly demarcated rectangles, as if she were defying the suggested portions.

'Maybe it's some kind of primordial desire.' Rolling up his pyjama sleeves, Izumi stepped into the kitchen. 'I'm going to make some coffee. Want any?'

'Sorry, these days the smell of coffee makes me sick.'

'A chocoholic who can't stand coffee. Seems like a contradiction, doesn't it?'

'Yeah, sorry.'

Since then, Izumi had avoided making coffee when Kaori was around.

While waiting for the water to boil, he threw some coffee beans from the freezer into the grinder and pressed the switch. It was taking a long time for him to use up these light-roast beans, a gift from a junior colleague who'd bought them while attending a business event in Seattle.

Breakfast was always toast and eggs with a salad or fruit juice on the side, and their unspoken rule was that the first person up made breakfast. When he'd lived with his mother, breakfast had always been rice and pickles with a side of something like grilled fish or fried egg. Yuriko was constantly on the go, either working or doing the housework, and on weekdays, she occasionally bought assorted sushi packs or sides from the deli counter at the supermarket for supper. Izumi looked forward to those times when she brought home readymade food. But soon after he got married, Yuriko told Kaori she'd always felt bad about serving her son anything bought pre-prepared. 'That's why I tried to at least make him breakfast and a packed lunch every day.'

He remembered the three loaves of bread beside his mother's rice cooker. He wondered when she'd started eating toast for breakfast. How long after he'd left home? Sitting down at the dining table, he broke the yolk of his sunny-side-up egg with his chopsticks. He popped a piece of egg in his mouth, then took a bite of toast and a sip of coffee.

'I have to leave early tomorrow to take the cellist from New York to an interview.' The words Kaori had said the night before came back to him. The dose of caffeine, his first in a while, must have set his brain working because he remembered she'd also said, 'Be sure to tell your mother about the baby, okay?' Kaori was almost four months pregnant now, but somehow Izumi hadn't got round to telling his mother.

Glancing out the window, he saw it was snowing. Even though it's already March, he thought glumly. Their third-floor apartment looked down on a large park. The falling snow looked like a profusion of white blossoms bursting from a lush green grove.

He took an almost-too-hot shower to warm himself up before leaving for work. A thin layer of snow topped the safety railing in front of the entrance. He scooped some up with both hands and squeezed. The snowball made a scrunching sound as it formed into a moist clump. He liked snow, but found the cold sensation in his hand right now unpleasant.

He would have to send an apology once he reached the office. The thought arose as the coldness in his fingertips reached his brain. The theme song for that TV show. The scriptwriter, one with whom Izumi was on friendly terms, had wanted to use an American pop song, but the copyright owner, who lived in the States, had yet to respond to Izumi's many emails, and negotiations had got bogged down. Three months without any progress.

His sigh turned to a white cloud in front of him – his funk made visible. As if bracing himself, he took a deep breath of cold air and set off. He called his mother on the way but her phone switched instantly to voicemail. He hung up without leaving a message.

As a child, he'd often played in the snow with the neighbourhood children. Whenever it snowed, he would dash from the house and head for the park. They would spend an hour, then another, having snowball fights, and when they tired of that, build countless snowmen. Yuriko couldn't afford to take long holidays, so Izumi had rarely gone on any trips. That's why he loved it when it snowed; the familiar town became a different place.

'One of the boys at school went to Akita with his family. His dad made him a *kamakura*, and they ate *oshiruko* inside it.' Izumi still couldn't forget the look on Yuriko's face when he had said this. He'd only meant to share his wonder at the idea of building a *kamakura*, a shelter made by hollowing out a mound of packed snow, but he had mentioned the word 'dad.' He'd said it like an insinuation, even though he must have known it would hurt his mother; even though he should have been used to holding back.

When he woke the next day, there was a mound of snow in the garden. Still in pyjamas, he shoved his feet into a pair of outdoor sandals and ran into the yard.

'Wow! Cool! What's going on?!'

'I made it for you,' his mother said.

'Can I go inside?'

'Of course, but carefully!'

The *kamakura* Yuriko had spent the night gathering snow to make was barely big enough for Izumi to fit inside, but it was a beautiful rounded shape, like a soft, plump mochi stuffed with sweet bean paste.

Leaving Izumi to revel in the snow hut, Yuriko went inside and began making *oshiruko*. She coughed occasionally as she stirred the pot of sweet adzuki bean soup over the flame. Hearing his mother through the glass patio door, Izumi called out after each cough to ask if she was all right, but she shouted back that she was fine and kept on stirring.

Izumi ate his sweet bean soup while curled up inside the icy shelter. Chunks of grilled rice cake floated in the thick reddish-brown broth. Yuriko sat outside, sipping from her bowl while her nose turned crimson. That night, they both came down with high fevers. Placing their futons side by side, they lay down. The *oshiruko* was so good, wasn't it, they giggled.

'Mum, I'm sorry. I don't need a dad. All I need is you.'

I finally said it, Izumi thought with relief, but it was just a fever-driven dream, and he woke to find his mother in the kitchen making rice porridge.

Thick flakes of snow were falling.

Izumi picked up his pace. Another memory came back as if in time with the rhythm of his pulse.

Once, before Izumi was old enough to start school, Yuriko had sat him in the child seat on the back of her bike and headed off for the stadium. Izumi had begun to take an interest in baseball, and she must have wanted to show him a real game. They reached the stadium by the sea after thirty minutes or so, but couldn't find the bicycle parking, and his mother circled the outside of the stadium as dusk began to fall. Izumi watched perspiration spread across his mother's back, drenching her shirt as she pedalled. They had circled the stadium once and were half way around again when bright field lights switched on and the game started. A roar rose from the crowd. Perhaps the first batter got a hit. Izumi raised his face. Cheering voices seemed to rain down from the sky.

The snow was falling more thickly. He'd been too lazy to bring an umbrella, but now he regretted it. He didn't feel like walking all the way to the subway station so he walked as far as the main road and tried to hail a cab. Normally there would be plenty of empty taxis coasting by, but this morning they were all full.

Feeling the snowball melting slowly in the palm of his hand, Izumi let his imagination roam. If they had a boy, would he make him a snow hut? Would they play catch together? Would he teach him how to fish or build a fire with him at a campground? Would he one day listen to his son's troubles at work over a drink?

I have a feeling it's a boy, Kaori had murmured last weekend as they lay in bed with the lights out. Guess I better start practising baseball then, Izumi responded, pitching his voice at the same decibel level. The next day on a whim, he dropped into a sporting goods store near his office, but there was such a surprising variety of glove shapes, he fled, not knowing what to choose.

'Honestly!' grumbled Tanijiri. 'The place they sent me is a nightmare!'

He munched on a small dish of salad. The voice issuing from his large, tanned frame was gruff. Izumi slathered his own salad with sesame dressing.

'Really?' Izumi said. 'But you're great with new talent. The job should be interesting.'

'Hah! That's what you think. It's a different era.'

'I guess you're right. Our contract terms are so severe now, we can't even get new talent to sign with us. We have to acquire artists who've already been successfully marketed.' Izumi glanced up from his salad and saw an uncomfortable-looking Tanijiri wiping sweat from his brow with a paper napkin. The temperature in this restaurant was always extreme. Too cold in summer, too hot in winter.

'There're so many ways artists can sell themselves these days anyway. No one needs to sign with a major label.'

'Don't give up on us yet!'

Until a few years earlier, Tanijiri and Izumi had worked at the same label. It handled a wide range of artists, from bands that released consecutive hits, to techno groups popular overseas. Tanijiri had been both a production director and a company executive. Although he was a first-rate creator, he lacked managerial talent. When the company's overall business performance deteriorated, he was demoted and transferred to an associate company involved in scouting and nurturing new talent. Brusque in manner and self-reliant, Tanijiri had made many enemies within the company, but he'd taught Izumi pretty much everything about the job – from how to deal with artists to making contacts in the business. When Tanijiri called out of the blue to say he was in Ichigaya for a meeting that had been cancelled due to snow and asked if Izumi had time to grab lunch, Izumi had dashed from the office to a nearby restaurant where they now sat across from each other.

'Besides, TV and movie producers aren't interested in trying out new talent.' Tanijiri stabbed at the salad remaining on his plate. The fork clutched in his thick fingers looked tiny. The lettuce looked like it had been in the fridge too long.

'You're right. I don't think producers even listen to music. They're always suggesting bands that were popular in the nineties.'

A waiter served them each a heaping plate of rice and a bowl of miso soup, which came with their meals. Izumi moved his soup off to one side. Tanijiri grinned as he crunched on an ice cube fished up from the bottom of his glass.

'You still hate miso soup, do you?'

'Yeah, sorry.'

'Doesn't bother me. It's just you're the only person I know who can't stand it. You're weird.'

'I just can't.'

The waiter returned, placing a heavy-looking cast iron platter in front of each of them, as though to obstruct their conversation. The well-grilled Hamburg steaks sizzled, spitting oil.

'Is TV production still under the sway of talent agencies?' asked Tanijiri.

'It's a bit better, but not much. Agencies still don't get it. They can push networks to use their musicians all they want, but if the artists don't have what it takes, they won't sell for long.'

Tanijiri fastened the paper bib around his neck. 'Same old story, huh?' he muttered with a grimace.

'Yeah. Nothing we can do about it though,' said Izumi, following suit with his own bib.

Deep creases lined Tanijiri's neck. He had played rugby in high school, making it all the way to the national championships, and his once-muscular neck was still as thick as a log. 'Tell me, who are you guys pushing now?'

'Ongaku, I guess.'

'Oh yeah, I heard they were joining. Even though they were selling fine as an indie band.'

'I was told it's because they like quite a few artists on our label.'

'So, bands are still drawn by that kind of thing, huh?'

'It looks like we'll be pushing their music for the theme song of Mr Komiyama's upcoming drama.'

'Oh-ho! Your old buddy, Mr Komiyama. You guys still play mahjong?' He flicked his wrists as though flipping over a row of mahjong tiles, then began carving up his Hamburg steak with the edge of his fork.

'Not anymore. What decade are you living in?' Rather than using his fork, Izumi split open a pair of chopsticks. The aroma of sizzling meat whetted his appetite.

'Who's in charge?'

'Tanabe.'

'Ah, the sexy one.'

'You know her?'

'She's going out with Osawa, the head of your department, right?'

'She is? Seriously?' Izumi glanced around quickly. Although it was still midday, the restaurant was dimly lit. The plain wooden tables were now full of customers, but he didn't see anyone from the office.

'Don't tell me you didn't know? I heard that like half a year ago.'

'So that's why Osawa always goes easy on Tanabe,' Izumi said in a hushed voice. He spread grated daikon evenly over the surface of his Hamburg steak. He'd never been much good at keeping up with in-house gossip and was always the last one to know things like this.

'That guy's so transparent,' said Tanijiri with a bark of laughter.

'Isn't that normal?'

'Far from it. If I were having an affair with someone in the office, I'd give them the cold shoulder in public or transfer them to a different department. It's too much trouble to try and cover up, right?'

'Very thoughtful of you.'

'Just call me an honest guy. Oh, here comes the wife who's good at her job.'

Izumi turned. From the entrance, Kaori raised a hand in greeting. She was with someone from the accounting department who'd joined the company at the same time as her. Izumi couldn't see Kaori's expression because she was backlit by the glass door, but her silhouette clearly showed the slight swelling of her abdomen. Catching sight of Tanijiri sitting across from her husband, Kaori inclined her head in greeting. Tanijiri gazed at her, acknowledging her by raising the hand that gripped his fork.

'So, you're going to be a daddy soon, are you?' he murmured. He'd been single since his divorce ten years ago. His child lived with his ex. Every time they went drinking, he would tell Izumi he couldn't get fired because at the very least he had to make his child support payments.

'In five months. Although it's still hard to believe.'

'You'll do fine. You look like the type who'll do just fine.'

'I wonder,' Izumi said absently, wishing he knew what Tanijiri meant by 'do just fine'. But the question, he realised, was meaningless.

The rice was starting to dry out on the flat plate. Izumi scooped up a mouthful.

As he walked home that snowy night, all sound seemed to fade away. As if everyone in the neighbourhood had vanished. Uneasy, he stood still in the silence. Did everyone feel this way? Or was it just him?

When he reached home, Kaori was already in bed. He opened his laptop on the dining table and began responding to the emails piled up in his inbox. Before he knew it, it was the middle of the night. When they first married, he and Kaori used to work overtime at home together, but when Kaori got pregnant, she started going to bed before midnight. I'm so sleepy, she would say. I need to get enough shuteye for two now. The way she smiled as she said this made Izumi feel like he'd touched some part of the joy that would come from having children.

In the middle of a huge yawn, Izumi was distracted by a mechanical buzz. The judder of his phone rippled towards him through the table. He grabbed it and looked at the screen. Yuriko Kasai.

'Hi? Mum?'

'Izumi? Sorry. Did you call me?'

'Yes but . . . It's so late.'

'Really? What time is it?'

'One thirty.'

The silence on his end was echoed on the other. An image rose in his mind: his mother in the living room with the grand piano, the smartphone she still hadn't got the hang of pressed against her ear. The only sound that reached him was the murmur of her voice. 'Sorry. Were you already in bed?'

'I was working.'

'Don't overdo it.'

'You too, Mum. You're up late.'

'Sometimes I wake up in the middle of the night. I just remembered that you called . . . Did something happen?'

Even if it had, why would you call me so late? You could've waited until morning. Words of reproach rose in his throat, but he held them back. 'There's something I wanted to tell you, Mum,' he said.

'What?'

Izumi paused, uncertain whether this was the right time.

'We're expecting.'

'Expecting?'

'Kaori and me. We're expecting a baby.'

'What? Congratulations! When's the due date?'

He could hear her voice rise slightly.

'August. I think.'

'I'm so happy for you. How's Kaori?'

'She's doing fine.'

'That's wonderful. Izumi, really, congratulations.' Her voice was trembling.

'And . . . when's it due,' she asked again.

'I already told you, in August,' he said.

'Oh, that's right. Very soon, isn't it? You'll need to get things ready.' As he listened to his mother's voice, Izumi relaxed, relieved to have finally told her.

When he'd announced his engagement to Kaori, Yuriko had fallen silent. Thinking that she was worried about what kind of partner he'd chosen, Izumi explained that they worked at the same company, yet his mother still said nothing. Trying to fill the awkward silence, he had babbled on about Kaori's personality and what she looked like, when suddenly his mother blurted out, 'It's so sudden.' As Izumi fumbled for words, his mother began to sob, drowning out his voice.

'We were just getting started,' she said, sniffing back tears. 'Up until now I had to focus all my energy on surviving. I thought that now we could finally go travelling or out for meals together. That I'd finally be able to do all the things parents usually do with their children.'

Izumi had thought his mother would be thrilled. Baffled to hear her pouting like a little child, he hadn't known what to say. A few weeks later, he introduced her to Kaori at a restaurant in Tokyo. She was in a much better mood and told Kaori embarrassing tales from Izumi's childhood. 'When he's grumpy, it's usually because he's hungry, so just give him something to eat,' she advised, adding, 'Anything will do.' And she and Kaori had laughed together.

That was already three years ago. Izumi had given Yuriko a Swiss watch as if in apology. A replacement for the old one he'd noticed she'd been using ever since he could remember.

Izumi looked at the clock on the wall and saw it was past two in the morning. His mother rambled on about one topic after another: the obstetrician, baby clothes, baby food, and bedtime routines. Occasionally, she stopped to murmur, Congratulations, Izumi, as though remembering. As he listened to her high-pitched voice, he was seized with the thought that his mother was going somewhere far away. Like that time.

4

Applause rose to the ceiling, bouncing off the timbers.

The cellist waited for the echoes to subside before commencing his first piece: Bach's Cello Suite No. 1 in G Major. The spotlights illuminated his large, tuxedoed frame. Izumi could feel the eyes of the full-house audience zeroing in on this single point. At the centre of the vast stage, foregrounded by the enormous pipe organ rising behind him, the cellist closed his eyes and raised his bow.

The repetitive, somehow plaintive melody. The resonant timbre of the cello, free and easy yet with a clear core running through it. Izumi had heard that the cello was similar in range to the male voice and that its tone sounded like human words. As he listened to the music filling the hall, it did indeed seem as if the cellist were singing.

'The cello has a solemn tone, which can make it sound rather gloomy,' Kaori had said that morning as she sat at the table munching chocolate. 'But the way this cellist plays is upbeat and relaxed. He's so good, he makes it look effortless. Even though he's an incredibly intelligent performer who thoroughly studies the score.'

Yuriko, who was sitting beside Izumi, took out her handkerchief after the cellist had only played the first three bars. Pushing up her glasses, she dabbed her left eye, then her right. I'm a bit of a crybaby these days, she had told him in the cab on the way to the concert hall. She'd been talking about a television drama she liked. He had rarely seen his mother cry, even when they lived under the same roof. Soon after he started elementary school, Izumi had made friends with one of the kids who lived on his route home from school, a boy named Miura.

Miura's parents worked, so no one was home during the day. As they were both latchkey kids, Izumi and Miura naturally became friends, and Izumi often spent evenings at the boy's house.

One day after school, just before winter holidays, Izumi was at Miura's as usual. They watched some anime and played cards, by which time the sun sinking in the west had begun to slant through the windows. Its orange light bathed the living room, which was scattered with toys and laundry. Miura looked towards the window.

'I'm hungry. How 'bout you?' he said, squinting his eyes against the blinding brightness.

'Uhm, yeah, I guess,' Izumi agreed. Miura wrapped an arm around his shoulders and said they should go and buy some sweets.

'But I don't have any money,' Izumi protested. He got less allowance than any of his friends.

'No problem. I know where Mum hides some.'

Miura went into the dining room and yanked open the right-hand drawer of the dish cabinet. Hidden under a pile of receipts for gas and electricity payments were two 1,000 yen notes and two 5,000 yen notes. Some coins also lay haphazardly in the drawer. Izumi's eyes grew round at the sight of such a huge sum of money treated so casually.

'Take as much as you like,' grunted Miura, grabbing a 1,000 yen note and crumpling it in his fist.

'No thanks,' said Izumi.

'Come on! Take some!'

'No, I don't need any.' Izumi knew this was wrong. He'd heard of such things as thieves. He knew the word 'stealing' too.

'If you don't, you're not my friend anymore!' Miura shouted. 'Hurry up and take it! If I say it's okay, then it's okay!'

Intimidated by Miura's ferocious expression, Izumi thrust his hand into the drawer. He grasped a 500 yen coin and shoved it in his pocket. The metal felt cold against his thigh. Miura opened the door, and light stabbed Izumi's eyes. He dashed down the stairs as if trying to dodge the light.

When they reached the supermarket, Miura headed straight for the sweet section. Izumi trotted after him as he passed along shelves filled with colourful bags of snacks. There was a marble-sized hole just under the arm of Miura's navy-blue sweater.

Miura threw chocolate bars, cola-flavoured gummies, fizzy candy, and other sweets into the basket. Turning to Izumi, he grinned and said, 'Pick whatever you like.' Izumi fixed his eyes on a bag of strawberry-milk sweets. Deep red strawberries printed on white plastic film. He loved those sweets. Fearfully, he took a bag and headed for the checkout counter.

Into his pocket went the change – a few 100-yen and 10-yen coins. In the end, he didn't eat the sweets at Miura's house. Instead, they split one of the chocolate bars Miura had bought. It had no flavour, and the viscous texture lingered in Izumi's mouth forever. Sitting beside him watching TV, Miura didn't look like he was enjoying his half either.

Izumi took the bag of strawberry-milk sweets home. 'Where did these come from?' Yuriko asked when she came back. When he didn't answer, she stopped washing the dishes and said sharply, 'Come on, out with it!' Bursting into tears, Izumi took the change from his pocket, placed it on the table and confessed his crime.

Yuriko took Izumi to Miura's house to return the money and the sweets. Miura was still alone, even though it was already dark. Yuriko bowed in apology and handed him the sweets and 500 yen. He took them with a sad look, his eyes on Izumi. 'Come over and play tomorrow,' he said with a smile.

Izumi walked home in the dark with his mother. He was longing to apologise, but didn't know how to put his feelings into words. His mother had said nothing since they left Miura's house. Was she still mad at him? He glanced up uneasily, and saw she was weeping. Stifling her sobs, she wiped her eyes with the back of her hand repeatedly.

That was the first time he'd seen his mother cry. She looked like a totally different woman. It frightened him, like seeing a hard shell cracked open and something soft oozing out. 'I'm sorry,' Izumi apologised, his voice trembling, and his mother patted him on the top of his head with her lily-white hand. Even now, the sweet fragrance of strawberry-milk sweets brought back that caress.

The cellist performed all six suites for solo cello with two intermissions in between. After playing the final phrase, he rose to his feet, drenched in sweat like a warrior after a long battle, and smiled as if with relief. The thunderous applause continued unabated, and he returned to the stage twice, then once more, bowing deeply each time. Izumi glanced at his mother. Tears flowed unchecked down her cheeks as she clapped.

Dressed in a suit, Kaori met them in the lobby. 'Did you enjoy it?' she asked Yuriko. Knowing that she loved Bach, Kaori had invited her to the concert about a week earlier.

'Oh yes, he was excellent, and he played with such freedom and ease,' Yuriko replied. She smiled bashfully as she wiped her moist eyes with her handkerchief. 'Thank you so much, Kaori.'

'I'm glad you liked it,' said Kaori.

'We're going out for dinner together. Want to join us?' Izumi asked. Looking apologetic, she said she had to stay for the post-concert signing session.

'I'll catch up with you when I'm finished,' she added.

'Okay. We'll be waiting for you.'

Kaori bowed to Yuriko, then hurried back to the sales booth. Noting her heelless leather pumps, Izumi felt a twinge of anxiety. Even from his vantage point on the sidelines, she had clearly been swamped since the cellist's arrival in Japan a few days earlier. For the last three days, she'd accompanied him to interviews, attended rehearsals, and prepared CDs for spot sales; late last night, she'd been on the phone to his manager checking up on his condition. Whenever Izumi told her to take care of herself, she gave him a thumbs up and said it was demanding, but it was her last big job.

Izumi and Yuriko exited the concert hall. An elevated expressway covered the sky. They were right at the junction of two major thoroughfares, and the curved concrete structures looked like giant arms. They walked a short distance through a cluster of skyscrapers and entered a bustling bistro. When they ate out, they always ended up at *yōshoku* restaurants serving European- and American-influenced cuisine, rather than traditional Japanese. A remnant of their custom of celebrating every special occasion together at Western-style diners and chain restaurants.

'How are your piano classes going?'

They sat at a table, and Izumi ordered a beer for himself and mineral water for Yuriko. When he was a child, students had come non-stop to their house for lessons, and the sound of the piano was always in the background. The melodies drifting up from the floor below seemed to declare his mother was not his alone.

Yuriko glanced around nervously, as if unused to being in a crowded restaurant.

'I've cut down the number I teach,' she said.

'Why?'

'I get tired so fast. Just one or two students a day and I feel exhausted.'

'Why don't you quit teaching then? You've got your pension, and I can increase the amount I send you.'

'Oh, but if I don't do something . . . I'll become useless.'

Izumi didn't know how to respond. Just like toys or machines, people became useless. His eyes fell on her hands, folded one on top of the other as if to hide her wrinkled skin.

With impeccable timing, the waiter placed a beer and a mineral water on the table, and Izumi hastily opened the menu. He ordered whatever caught his eye: a tomato and cheese salad, octopus carpaccio, ratatouille, assorted sausages. 'Tell me if there's anything you want to order,' he said, but Yuriko said she would leave it up to him.

'I really like my students. They're so sweet. Like Miku.'

'Miku?'

'She's in elementary school. She's learning to play 'Träumerei'. She keeps getting stuck on the second bar. You need to watch those notes, "do" and "fa."'

Tilting her head to one side, she tapped her fingertips on the gingham-covered table. Ton-ton.

'The other day,' Izumi said, then paused to take a sip of beer. 'It was pretty late when you called me, wasn't it?'

Yuriko looked at him as though startled from a dream. 'I'm sorry. For calling so late at night.'

'No problem. I was working anyway. But I wondered if you're having trouble sleeping.' He'd been worried about this ever since. Falling asleep was the one thing his mother had always been good at.

'Well, maybe a little. Sometimes I just wake up, that's all.' She waved her hand in front of her as if to dispel his concern. 'But I'm getting plenty of sleep. Why, today I didn't wake up until past noon!' She giggled.

'I see,' Izumi said. 'But I worry, you know. You should take care of your health.'

'I will,' Yuriko said. 'After all, I'm not getting any younger.'

'That's right,' Izumi said.

'But I'm okay,' she insisted. 'Really.'

'Why's that?' asked Izumi.

'I've been feeling great recently.'

'How come?'

She looked straight at him, her face brimming with confidence. 'I've been drinking something good.'

'It's not something fishy, is it?' Izumi returned her gaze, but her eyes flitted back and forth.

'Of course not. It's bona fide.'

The roar of cars reached Izumi's ears. He felt sure the expressway above the bistro was creaking and shuddering. Yuriko took a sip of water and began slowly telling him the story.

Two months earlier, a middle-aged woman in a white suit had come to Yuriko's front door. 'I'm surveying the water system in this area. Would you be willing to answer a questionnaire?' she asked with a smile. Behind her stood a young man in a navy blazer with a notebook in his hand. He was with her as a trainee, the woman explained. They looked respectable, and when the woman asked if they could come inside, Yuriko let them in.

The woman in the white suit and the young trainee sat side by side at the table. Yuriko sat across from them and filled out the questionnaire. As she answered simple questions about her diet, sleep patterns, health, and medications, the woman flashed another smile and said, 'Your handwriting is so beautiful.' Her complexion was fair, and her cheeks were smooth and firmly toned.

Once Yuriko finished, the woman asked, 'Which prefecture in Japan do you think has the dirtiest water?'

'Tokyo? Or maybe Osaka?' Yuriko responded.

The young man had been taking notes throughout. He seemed very thin, and his gold-buttoned blazer looked loose and baggy.

'And do you know which has the cleanest water?'

'Niigata perhaps. Or Hokkaido?'

'Did you know that water purity is closely related to beauty and longevity?' Without answering any of her own questions, the white-suited woman took out a thick binder. Neatly filed inside were a newspaper clipping introducing the health benefits of hydrogen, a magazine column on a famous baseball player who drank hydrogen water as part his routine, and a fashion magazine feature about an actress who had successfully lost weight drinking hydrogen water.

'I slimmed down quite a bit too,' the white-suited woman continued as she flipped through the pages. 'Cooking with hydrogen water makes food taste so much better. It cuts down the number of calories in the food and keeps you from overeating. Plus, it helps dissolve fat in your body, which is also good for weight loss.'

After listing off all the benefits of hydrogen water – how she no longer caught colds or got a stiff neck, how it reduced wrinkles and was a good make-up remover too, the white-suited woman suddenly laughed and closed the binder. 'I'm sorry. I got so carried away. You must think this is all rather dubious, right?'

'Oh no, not at all.' Yuriko shook her head. The young man kept his eyes on his notebook, taking notes. The only sound in the late-afternoon of the dining room was the scritch-scratch of his pen racing across the paper.

'Why don't you taste some and see?' said the woman, at which point, the sound of the pen stopped. From a small suitcase, the young man took out a machine that resembled a coffee maker. The woman pulled a bottle of mineral water from her bag, poured the contents into the machine's transparent tank, and pressed the switch. Bubbles began to rise, turning the water inside the tank cloudy. Yuriko watched with a thrill of excitement; it was like a science experiment. After about three minutes, the woman flicked off the switch and poured the water from the machine into a plastic cup.

'Drink this and compare it with the water from your tap,' she said. Yuriko poured herself a cup of water from the water purifier in the kitchen and compared it with the freshly made 'hydrogen water'. 'Delicious, right?' the woman said, and Yuriko nodded. She felt the hydrogen water was softer with a touch of sweetness.

The woman placed another binder on the table and opened it, saying that here was a newspaper clipping from just a few days ago. The young man beside her leaned forward and peered at it, taking notes, as if he was seeing it for the first time.

'It introduces a study on the effects of hydrogen water on mice by a renowned medical professor, scientifically proving the anti-ageing effects on the brain,' the white-suited woman said. She smiled for the third time that day.

'That sounds very suspect to me,' said Izumi accusingly. He downed a glass of red wine. 'To come so well prepared, bringing all those clippings.' A plate of sautéed pork he hadn't managed to finish lay in front of him. 'I think she's taking advantage of you.'

'That's not true. I really do feel great.'

'What about her claim that it helps cut calories in food? Where's her evidence?'

'But I have lost a little weight. And I haven't caught a cold recently.'

'And asking to come inside just to do a survey of the water system. That's suspicious right there.'

'But when I compared it to—'

'Mum, I'm telling you – you're being conned!' His voice was sharp, cutting her off. He couldn't bear the thought that his mother was being had. She'd always been good-natured, buying cookware and pots she didn't need because she couldn't refuse someone's request, or taking on the hardest jobs for the PTA at school. Whenever he saw this, Izumi felt his mother was being used. Why did she always take on such jobs? Couldn't she live her life more intelligently? At the very least, he wished she would avoid drawing the short end of the stick.

'If it makes you feel good, what could be better?' Kaori interjected, unable to bear it any longer. She'd joined them just as Yuriko had begun talking about hydrogen water and had sat beside her, listening. 'Izumi, you've had too much to drink,' she said.

'But those claims sound too good to be true.'

'I'm sure a lot of it has to do with how a person feels about it. Like the placebo effect.'

'Right, placebos. I find things like that hard to believe.'

'It doesn't really matter, does it? As long as it works.'

Izumi saw that his mother was pressing her handkerchief against her eyes again. 'I'm so sorry, Izumi,' she stammered, forcing each word out slowly. 'I didn't mean to make you worry. Or you, Kaori. I'm sorry. But it really is true. I'm feeling much better now. I don't catch colds anymore, and the pain in my knee is gone. So, it's okay if I keep drinking it, right?'

Not knowing what to say to his mother who had suddenly become so prone to tears, Izumi shut up. Kaori caught his eye, and gave him a fierce look as if urging him to change the subject. Galvanised by the cheerful jazz tune playing in the background, Izumi said brightly, 'Mum, about our conversation on the phone the other night.'

'What? Phone?'

'You called me late at night, remember?'

'Oh yes, I did.'

'Well, about the baby.'

'Baby? What baby?'

'Come on, Mum. I told you on the phone. We're going to have a baby.'

A puzzled smile spread across Yuriko's face. Was she pretending she'd forgotten, he wondered. Or was she just not ready to accept it yet? Kaori glared at him accusingly and tugged his sleeve.

'Didn't you tell her?'

'Of course I did,' Izumi said, and turned back to Yuriko. 'Stop it, Mum,' he said.

'Oh, yes . . . now I remember.' The blank look on her face wavered, and she clapped her hands. 'Kaori, Izumi, congratulations!'

Kaori inhaled sharply and stared at her mother-in-law. Listening to the dry sound of his mother's applause, Izumi recalled the chill of snow spreading across the palm of his hand.

5

'Saying you forgot won't get you off the hook,' Osawa growled as he left the meeting room. His eyes were badly bloodshot. He was always foul-tempered in the morning. As the head of their department, he spent much of his time dining and drinking late into the night with TV directors and talent agency reps.

'But like I said,' Tanabe protested in a nasal voice, 'I didn't forget.' She trotted after him. A black flared skirt and enamel heels; wavy chestnut hair tied back with a scrunchy, and a turtleneck jumper that showed off her curves. Her feminine attire was a stark contrast to the hoodies and jeans the rest of the staff wore.

'Stop making excuses!' Osawa snapped without looking at her.

'But I wasn't at the meeting when the decision was made.'

'And just what do you think the minutes are for? Read them!'

'I'm sorry,' Izumi interjected. 'I should've made sure she knew.' He didn't want to become involved, but he had to do something or this would drag on forever.

'Kasai, don't try to defend your staff. This one's under the mistaken impression that she's clever and gets things done efficiently.'

Realising that further protest would be counterproductive, Izumi swallowed his words.

The issue was a double booking. For Ongaku, the new indie band the company had lured to the label with a megabucks deal. The tie-in team was touting the band as one of its most promising groups and promoting it widely to producers of everything from TV shows to game apps. Thanks to these efforts, Komiyama, a well-known scriptwriter with whom Izumi had forged a close connection, had taken a liking to them. He agreed to use their new single as the theme song for his next TV series. Unaware of this development, Tanabe had approached one of the top film-production studios, and they wanted to use the single as the theme song for a movie being released during the winter holidays. 'They originally asked for an American pop song, but when I recommended Ongaku instead, they agreed,' Tanabe had proudly announced just before the meeting ended. Everyone else in the room froze.

In the hallway, Osawa finally turned and looked at Tanabe. 'Go and apologise right now,' he demanded.

Tanabe's eyes still seemed to plead that it wasn't her fault. 'I already emailed the film company. They replied right away.'

'What'd they say?'

'They want to talk to you. They said to put them in touch with the person in charge.'

'It's your mess – don't expect me to clean it up!' Osawa bellowed, just as the door to the lesson room at the end of the hall opened. A group of small teenage girls with towels around their necks scurried out like ants. Good morning, they said, one after the other as they passed. Covered in sweat and without any make-up, they didn't look at all like pop idols who could pack the Tokyo Dome.

Nagai, a relatively new employee, had been standing silently beside Izumi throughout this exchange. He wore a beanie with a skateboard logo, and an oversized hoodie. 'Why not try and make both projects work?' he muttered under his breath, then pulled his phone from his pocket and began fiddling with it.

'Mr Osawa, I'll talk to Mr Komiyama myself,' Izumi said. It was the only solution he could think of. 'And the TV producer as well.'

Nagai nodded as if to say, 'That's more like it.' His eyes were still glued to his phone.

Izumi suddenly wondered how the music video he'd put Nagai in charge of was going. He'd heard the production company's estimate was over budget, but no steps had been discussed for cutting costs. The director Nagai had brought in produced highly artistic work, but his production costs always exceeded the budget. If shooting was scheduled to start next week, how was Nagai planning to keep costs down? The realisation that Nagai might just be unrealistically optimistic was depressing.

Osawa, who was glaring at Tanabe, shifted his gaze to Izumi.

'You think that will solve it?'

'I won't know until I try, but they might agree if we can adjust the timing a little.'

'It would be good if we could do both – the movie and the TV series.'

'I think it's possible.'

'I'll leave it to you then.'

Osawa was fond of saying, 'Just give me the good news, will you?' He took on only sweet-sounding propositions, foisting anything troublesome onto his subordinates. He wasn't popular, but he'd never caused any major trouble either, and he was moving steadily up the corporate ladder. Before Tanijiri was transferred, he liked to say that the ones who survived in this company were those who didn't have anything they wanted to achieve.

Tanabe bowed to Izumi. 'I'm sorry, Mr Kasai. I'll go with you. When would be a good time?'

'The earlier the better, I guess. I'll check with the client, but how about tomorrow? It's a Saturday though.'

'That's fine.'

'Okay. Keep it open then.'

After thanking him, Tanabe smiled and bowed, then slung her high-end handbag over her shoulder and got in the lift. Izumi had planned to go to his mother's that weekend, but he'd have to postpone again. An image rose in his mind. His mother, sitting on a swing under a cold sky. What was happening to her?

The night of the cello concert, as they'd left the restaurant, she'd said, 'I'm sorry, Izumi. I'm getting a bit forgetful these days. I remember now. You did tell me. I was planning to ask you whether it's a boy or a girl.'

He'd been intending to visit her more often to check on how she was doing, but kept giving precedence to the work at hand.

'Geez. I wish they'd do that kind of thing in bed instead.'

Izumi was standing at the urinals when Nagai came up beside him, still clutching his phone. He swiftly typed a message one-handed while relieving himself.

'You knew?'

'You kidding? They've been an item for over half a year already.'

'I just heard the other day.'

'You're always so oblivious.' Nagai chuckled dryly, shoving his phone into his pocket and heading to the sink. 'Pretty much everyone knows.'

'They're so observant.'

'No, you just don't pay enough attention. I mean really, they take holidays on the same day and disappear from launch parties at the same time. Pretty obvious, isn't it? They could cover it up better than that.'

'Now you mention it, that's true,' Izumi said, standing at the next sink. The chattering of the idol group in the women's washroom next door permeated the wall. Their voices had a sultry tone that made it hard to believe they were the same girls who'd greeted them so demurely before.

'But I wish they'd cut it out.'

'What?' Izumi pressed the pump of the liquid soap dispenser and white foam spurted out.

'It's a drag having to pretend we don't know. Osawa is one thing, but everyone's always buttering up Tanabe too. How come the people having the affair are always the only ones who think no one knows what's going on? And that fight back there? It just looks like they're playing around.' As he expounded on this theme, Nagai looked into the mirror and adjusted his beanie. He almost never spoke up at meetings, but would suddenly get talkative at a pub or in the toilets like this. The way he spoke sounded as though he was talking to himself; Izumi often lost track of who Nagai was speaking to.

'That's considerate of everyone. To pretend they haven't noticed.'

'No, it isn't. They're just amusing themselves.'

'Amusing themselves?'

'They're watching from a safe distance, then using what they see as food for gossip. They're letting them get away with it because it's entertaining. Not me though.'

At the sight of Nagai's sober expression, Izumi thought of the smirks and knowing glances between his colleagues he had recently noticed when Osawa and Tanabe were talking to each other in the office. He knew he'd seen that kind of sneer before, and now he remembered where. It was the same look people had given his mother around that time.

The howl of a machine jolted him back to reality. Nagai had thrust his hands into the hand dryer. 'See you later,' he mumbled, exiting the toilets, his eyes already glued to the phone he'd pulled from his pocket again. Left alone, Izumi could hear the girls still chattering next door. Their voices ricocheted off the tile walls, echoing shrilly, almost like shrieks.

As they came round a long curve, a manmade beach came into view.

The train was packed with people who'd finished their Saturday shopping. Perhaps there was an anime event going on somewhere – Izumi was surrounded by cosplayers in turquoise or orange wigs mutely gripping the straps. The plastic seats were so small he felt like he was riding on playground equipment.

The night before, when he'd told Kaori he had to work in the morning, she'd sighed. 'You always do that, put things off,' she said sharply, without taking her eyes off the TV news.

'It can't be helped,' he replied, feeling a little guilty for having waited until the last minute to tell her. 'We've got a major problem at work.'

Kaori switched off the TV and stood up. 'You always act as though it's got nothing to do with you. Stop using work as an excuse and think about your mother for once, okay?' After spitting out these words, she marched into the bedroom and slammed the door.

'You're so kind, Izumi.' The soft voice came from beside him.

Until a moment ago, Tanabe had been writing in her emerald green diary, but now her eyes were on him. Greyish-brown eyes. Although it was still cold, she wore a thin sweater cut low at the neckline, accentuating her breasts, and a short, tight skirt. His eyes were drawn involuntarily to the whiteness of her neck. A slender rose-gold chain shone on her chest. 'I see you still use a real agenda, Tanabe,' said Izumi. He shifted his gaze discreetly to the green enamel cover.

'Yes. But so do you.'

Izumi and Tanabe were famous as the only two left in the department who weren't using Google calendar. Their co-workers kept begging them to hurry up and switch to the cloud because it was such a pain to coordinate their schedules otherwise, but they'd stubbornly stuck with paper.

'The idea of entrusting my memory or schedule to a machine or putting it online scares me. It goes against my nature.'

'I know what you mean. The other day I couldn't find my phone. It was terrifying.' Tanabe's grip on her diary tightened. 'I searched all over for a pay phone, but couldn't find one anywhere. Then, when I finally did, I couldn't remember anyone's phone number. Not my parents', my co-workers' or my friends'. The thought that I'd relinquished all my memories to something I only started using ten or so years ago was quite scary.'

Shutters clicked in rapid succession. The cosplayers had started a photo shoot in the train. Rather than pointing their camera phones at each other, they were taking selfies.

'Still, I suppose it's easier to put everything on the internet. There's no risk of losing it that way either. And everything can be shared.'

'I don't want to share,' Tanabe said. 'And the fact it stays online forever is a risk too, you know. Plus, there are some memories I'd rather delete.' Tanabe paused suddenly and shot Izumi a startled look. 'But I suppose if I had done that, this trouble would never have happened, would it,' she concluded with a frown.

'Well, it's partly my fault, for not telling you.'

'I'm sorry I got you in trouble too.' She bowed her head, and Izumi caught a whiff of jasmine. Perfume or shampoo? She must have known that everything from her clothes to her fragrance were all part of her arsenal.

'What did the film production people say?'

'They said it's okay as long as we can change the timing.'

'Mr Komiyama doesn't seem to mind either, so I guess we only have to convince the broadcaster.'

'That's a relief,' Tanabe said, her voice almost a whisper. Izumi's gaze kept being drawn back to her glossy pink lips.

The buzzer sounded, announcing the train's arrival at the next station, and the cosplayers all filed out onto the platform. In their place, several families with children who looked to be in elementary school got on. In the crowded train, Tanabe's soft thigh pressed against his leg.

'When did you get married?' Tanabe asked after a long pause.

'Two years ago.' Surprised by this sudden question, Izumi stared straight ahead as he answered her.

'What's it like? Being married to someone from the same company?'

'The fact we already knew each other makes it easy. But sometimes it's hard to get a break. Because we talk about work even at home.'

'I think that's great. That'd be my ideal,' said Tanabe. When she added 'And Kaori's lovely, isn't she,' Izumi almost asked, How about you, Tanabe, but caught himself in time. He recalled how Osawa had shouted at her to clean up her own mess. What expression had been on Osawa's face when he'd said that to her, Izumi wondered.

He said nothing, and Tanabe murmured in his ear, 'But didn't anyone in the company find out you were seeing each other?'

'Find out?'

'You must have been spotted on dates. Or seen leaving the office together.'

'We weren't particularly worried about people finding out, but even so, it seems nobody knew. Everyone looked shocked when we announced we were getting married.'

'Really? But maybe you just didn't realise that everyone knew already.'

Looking at her cheerful face, Izumi gave a crooked smile. 'Yeah, maybe,' he said.

When they heard the news, several of his co-workers had told him they were surprised Kaori had picked him. She was seen within the company as someone who put work first. Words like 'falling in love' or 'marriage' didn't fit her image, and certainly no one ever expected her to marry someone from the office.

That evening five years earlier in the barbecue restaurant when Izumi had confided he didn't have a father, he'd sensed that he would marry Kaori. She accepted his confession so readily that he felt he could spend his life with her without feeling shame or inferiority. But he had yet to ask her why she'd chosen him.

The phone gripped in his hand vibrated insistently. Glancing at the screen, he saw it was from a landline he didn't recognise. Filled with a sudden uneasiness, he answered, cupping a hand around his mouth.

'Is this Izumi Kasai?'

'Yes.'

'Yuriko Kasai's son?'

'Yes.'

The person was taking too long to tell him why they were calling; Izumi felt irritated. 'What is it?' he asked. 'What about by mother?'

'Well, you see, Yuriko is with us right now.'

'Yes, but where is that?'

'With the police.'

At the word police, the rattling of the shaking train seemed to fade, growing muffled. As he listened absently to the policeman and murmured appropriate responses, Izumi saw their destination come into view. The silver TV station rising from reclaimed land looked like an enormous spaceship.

An array of scattered colours greeted Izumi when he opened the door.

Everything from pumps to trainers and sandals were strewn across the entranceway. 'Sorry for the mess,' Yuriko said, darting in ahead of him to tidy them up. Their entrance way was so small, it had always been their rule to put the shoes away in the cabinet.

'You must be hungry,' she said. 'I'll make you something to eat.' She went into the kitchen and opened the fridge. The light of the setting sun shone through the living room window onto the well-worn grand piano. She had always kept it tuned and polished, but now it was covered with a thick layer of dust. The flower on the dining table had wilted, and the water in the vase was a murky brown. Only the laundry was neatly folded and stacked on the sofa.

'Just tea is fine. I'll grab something at the station before going home.' Having rushed straight to the police station from Daiba, he'd skipped lunch, but he didn't feel like eating.

'Don't say that. I'll whip up something right now.' He could see the exhaustion in her face, perhaps from her long stay at the police station, but her obsession with doing the right thing kept her standing in the kitchen.

Izumi came and stood beside his mother; he asked if he could give her a hand. She looked somehow vulnerable as she turned on the burner. He glanced at the sink and saw a burned pot soaking in water. How many times had she burned it, he wondered. The bottom and even the handle were charred black. The strainer basket for the sink was full of food scraps and stank of rotten fish. Three loaves of bread still sat by the rice cooker, just like the last time he'd come. He picked up the one at the back. It must have been quite old; the end piece was covered in mould. He threw the whole bag into the bin, then opened the fridge. There were two bottles each of ketchup and mayonnaise, all with their lids left open.

Izumi had hurried from the train station to the police *kōban* to find Yuriko sitting slumped in a plain folding chair. A middle-aged officer in uniform was sitting across from her, regarding her steadily. When Izumi was ushered into the room by a younger officer, he looked up and asked, 'You're her son?' then motioned him to the chair beside Yuriko.

'Mum, what's going on?' Izumi knew he sounded accusatory but he couldn't help it. Yuriko stared down at her lap without responding. Beside her was a white plastic bag from the supermarket in front of the station.

'The other party doesn't want to make a big deal of it.' The police officer smiled soothingly and began filling in the blanks on a form. Izumi wondered if this happened often. The suffocating closeness of the small room was relieved only by the faint scratching of the ballpoint pen and the ticking of the clock.

'Is everything paid for?' Izumi asked the officer. 'Mum, don't just sit there saying nothing. Tell me what happened!' Impatience made him speak in a rush.

But still she said nothing. In a slow, deliberate voice, as though trying to calm Izumi, the officer spoke for her. 'She had her wallet with her and paid for everything. It seems your mother walked around the supermarket for about two hours. One of the employees was puzzled by her behaviour. He kept an eye on her, and saw her put things like eggs, tomatoes, and mayonnaise in her bag. Then she started to walk out of the store without passing through the checkout counter. That's when she was stopped. But she doesn't seem to have meant any harm. She was confused, not sure how this could have happened. So, the store contacted us.'

After Izumi filled in the pertinent sections of various forms, he and Yuriko were freed. The officer smiled at Yuriko and urged her to be careful next time. The experience seemed to have dashed her spirits, because she never opened her mouth once, bowing repeatedly instead.

Waiting until Yuriko stepped outside the police *kōban*, the officer said quietly to Izumi, 'You might want to take your mother to the doctor.'

While Izumi washed the dishes in the sink, Yuriko took out a square frying pan. She poured beaten eggs into it, waited for the omelette to thicken, then rolled it up. Izumi's request. Just omelette is fine, he'd said.

'It's ready.' With this pronouncement, she slid the omelette onto a plate. Steam rose from the bright yellow mass.

'Looks delicious!' Izumi said. The sweet aroma had revived his appetite, and he went to the table. He split the omelette in two with his chopsticks and placed one half on his mother's plate. Yuriko poured hot water from the kettle into the teapot.

'That's so barbaric,' she said. 'I would have cut it for you with a knife.'

'Doesn't change the flavour,' Izumi responded, shoving a piece into his mouth. The omelette was still hot from the pan, and he rolled it around in his mouth to cool it down as he chewed. The creamy eggs melded with the sweetness of the sugar on his tongue.

His mother had always put this rolled omelette in the lunches she packed for school sports days or field trips. The sweetness made it seem like a dessert even though it was a side dish. When he was in high school, she had gone through a phase of trying to perfect it. She proudly told him she'd made her own soup stock from scratch using dried bonito flakes. This gave the omelette a more sophisticated, grown-up taste, but Izumi was soon longing for her customary sweet rolled omelette and asked her to go back to that. Ever since, the flavour had remained unchanged.

He polished off his portion in no time. It was just as soft and sweet as always. 'Delicious,' he said.

'That's good,' his mother said with a smile.

Although Izumi was sure his fears must be ungrounded, he still managed to say, 'Mum, let's go see the doctor next week.'

She nodded. 'Yes, let's do that.' She cut her share of the omelette in half and slipped the larger piece onto Izumi's plate.

6

'How old are you?'

'Sixty-eight.'

'What's the date today? And what day of the week?'

'April . . . eighth, Saturday.'

'Where are we?'

'The hospital.'

'Please repeat these three words after me and remember them. I'm going to ask you to tell me them again later. Cherry. Cat. Train.'

A young doctor with silver-rimmed spectacles fired off one question after another in a deep voice. Perhaps he played golf or tennis. His face was tanned, and his arms were powerfully muscled where they stuck out from his rolled-up sleeves.

'Cherry . . . Cat . . . Train.' Looking like a frightened little girl on her first visit to a hospital, Yuriko repeated the words hesitantly after the doctor.

'What's a hundred minus seven?'

'Ninety . . . three.'

'And if you subtract seven from that?'

'Eighty . . . umm . . .'

'You're on the right track, Mrs Kasai.'

'Eighty . . . six.'

You did it, Mum! Izumi almost blurted out. She was making a valiant effort, and he wanted to cheer her on. The blank white walls of the hospital examination room felt somehow claustrophobic. Izumi's clenched fists were slick with sweat. The doctor pushed up his glasses and continued without pause.

'Now please say these numbers backwards. Six, eight, two.'

'Two . . . eight . . . six?'

'Three, five, two, nine.'

'Umm . . . nine . . . two . . . five . . . sorry.'

'No problem. You're doing fine, Mrs Kasai. Now, please tell me the three words you memorised earlier.'

'Cat . . . train . . . uh . . . Oh, dear . . .' Yuriko looked at Izumi as if pleading for help. Through the window behind her, he could see cherry trees in full bloom. Please stop! These words almost escaped Izumi's throat. The doctor kept his eyes on Yuriko.

'How about it? Just one more word to go, Mrs. Kasai.'

'Cat . . . train . . . cat . . . It's no good. I can't remember.' Yuriko looked at Izumi, who said nothing, then turned and gave the doctor a weak smile. 'You don't have to be so mean, you know,' she teased, trying to laugh off her humiliation.

While Yuriko was getting a brain MRI, Izumi was called back into the examination room.

'I conducted a simple test on your mother earlier.'

'What do you think?'

'Considering her forgetfulness and the other symptoms she exhibited before coming here, I believe her dementia has progressed to some extent.' He spoke dispassionately, as if diagnosing a common cold; putting into words the very thing Izumi didn't want to acknowledge. Izumi shifted his gaze to stare blankly out the window. The cherry trees, blossoms at their peak, appeared naive and foolish. They displayed their blooms so proudly, ignorant of the fact those petals would soon fall.

'We'll have to conduct a thorough examination to determine the cause, but I suspect it's Alzheimer's. There are several other types of dementia, including Lewy body and cerebrovascular, but more than half of all cases are due to Alzheimer's.'

Izumi could not connect the word Alzheimer's with his mother. It sounded unreal, like a disease that infested a distant land from some fable.

'At this hospital, we prescribe Aricept or Reminyl for patients diagnosed with Alzheimer's. If these drugs work, they can delay its advancement, but even then, their effectiveness is temporary. From just a few months to up to five years. Nerve cells in the brain gradually die off, but we don't know the cause. It's believed that a certain type of protein is related to onset of the disease.'

The names of outpatients being summoned over the intercom echoed outside the room. So many diseases inside this building. When Izumi didn't respond, the doctor said slowly, 'Mr Kasai, please do your best to support your mother. Dementia's now quite common. The number of patients in Japan alone exceeds five million. In another eight years, it will be seven million, and we'll have entered an era in which one in five seniors have dementia.'

'So someday, wonder drugs will be developed, making it a curable disease? Like they're doing with cancer now?'

'Maybe. But ironically, it seems that humans are designed to keep a balance.'

'Balance,' Izumi repeated, as if to himself. Yuriko and Izumi. The balance they'd maintained thus far was about to crumble – again.

'The human life span used to be about fifty years. When it increased, people started getting cancer. When cancer became curable, people lived even longer, but there were more cases of Alzheimer's. It seems that no matter how far humans advance, we'll always have to fight against something.'

The doctor rose from his chair, telling Izumi that his mother would soon be back from the MRI. 'Just because she has dementia doesn't mean she'll forget everything or stop understanding,' he said. 'Yuriko Kasai is still your mother. Remember to treat her with love and respect.'

There was a timid knock. Just the thought of what must be going through his mother's mind as she waited outside the door made Izumi's heart ache. As he sat there unable to speak, the doctor, who up until now had been talking in a confidential tone, announced brightly, 'Please come in!'

The doctor showed Yuriko the MRI images and explained that she was in the early stages of Alzheimer's disease. She nodded without looking particularly surprised and said she understood. She didn't seem to grasp that the round slices of brain in the images were inside her own cranium.

In the cab, she said nothing the whole way home. Izumi couldn't find anything to say either, and they stared out the window, each on their own side. A spring breeze scattered the cherry petals from the trees lining the road up the hill to her house.

Yuriko made some *hōjicha*. While sipping the tea, they discussed what to do next. Izumi suggested getting care services or having her move in with them. Yuriko said she wanted to try living independently a little longer, but she seemed to be speaking without really knowing what to do. Izumi asked if there was anyone nearby who could help her, but she shook her head.

Yuriko had no relatives and almost no one she could call a friend. The longer she lived, the more alone she became. Perhaps that's what it means to approach the end of life, Izumi thought.

'I wonder if I should quit teaching.' His mother sat at the grand piano and pressed the keys as though checking to see if she could still play. Chopin's 'Minute Waltz'. She missed two or three notes at the beginning but quickly regained her touch. The pleasant sound of the piano resonated in the small room. 'I can still play perfectly well.'

Listening to the spritely tune, Izumi found it hard to believe his mother's brain was infirm. 'If you're worried, why don't you take a break for a while? You can always start up again once you're feeling better.'

Although he knew the chances were slim, he suggested it anyway, addressing his words to the back of her slight frame. Would she ever teach piano again?

'I just have one student now. Miku, the little girl who lives on the corner,' Yuriko said. 'I cut down the number of students because I was getting older. You're sending me money too, so I don't need to push myself.' She kept repeating this over and over as if trying to convince herself.

'Izumi,' she said as soon as she saw him. Then seeing his flustered expression, she laughed. 'I guess you don't recognise me, do you?' She pulled her long black hair up behind her head, drawing his attention to her almond-shaped eyes. Memory rushed back. Her face was plumper, but those eyes hadn't changed since junior high.

'Oh! Miyoshi!'

'Bingo. But my surname's Hasegawa now, not Miyoshi. Since I got married.'

'You mean you're Miku's mother?'

'That's right.' A grin spread across her face, and she opened the door wide to welcome him inside.

'How many years has it been?'

Sitting on the white fabric-covered sofa, Izumi glanced around the spotless living room. Although they lived on the same block, Miyoshi's house got more light than Yuriko's, where an apartment complex blocked the sky.

'I haven't seen you since we graduated from senior high,' Miyoshi said. 'Which means it must be about twenty years.' Her slippers flapped against the floor as she padded over and placed a tray in front of Izumi. The tea in the flower-patterned teacups must have been scented. Izumi caught the sweet aroma of caramel.

'I didn't realise you lived so close.'

'I got married as soon as I graduated from junior college. My husband works at a bank and his parents let us have their house. It's been eight years since Miku was born.'

The sound of a piano came from the child's room. Mozart's 'Turkish March'. It must have been a practice piece. She kept getting stuck at the same place. Each time she stopped and started over from the beginning.

'You're already a mother. But you haven't changed a bit.'

'That's not true. I've gained weight. It's awful. How about you?'

'We're going to have a baby in August.'

'Your first?'

'Uh-huh. I'm completely clueless, so it's quite a steep learning curve. My wife's been pretty grumpy lately,' he said with a rueful grin. He sipped his tea.

'You look like you'll do fine, Izumi.'

'People often tell me that, but I don't know why.'

'You're the one who hasn't changed, Izumi. You were always so grown up.'

'Well, I was raised by a single mother. But you should have told me your daughter was learning piano from my mum.'

'I didn't know your number. Were you surprised?'

'Sure was.'

'I've admired your mother ever since junior high,' Miyoshi murmured, then stopped to listen to her daughter playing. She was still getting stuck at the same spot. Miyoshi continued in the same husky voice Izumi remembered. 'Mrs Kasai. She was such a beautiful, classy woman, and so good at piano. I always wanted to take lessons from her. It was too late for me, but now my daughter's learning.'

'I never knew that. I guess I really am oblivious.'

'Why do you say that?'

'Everyone says so,' Izumi said wryly. 'I look like I ought to be good at things, but in fact I'm pretty dense.'

Izumi had been fourteen when he and his mother moved into this neighbourhood. Yuriko had managed to purchase a small house with a living room just big enough to fit the grand piano. It was an old house, twenty minutes on foot and uphill from the nearest station, which meant that even Yuriko could afford it if she took out a mortgage. She intended to advertise for new students and teach piano once they moved in.

On the day Izumi changed schools, his homeroom teacher introduced him to the class and pointed out his seat. Walking down the aisle of the unfamiliar classroom, he heard someone say, 'Izumi Kasai.' At the desk beside his sat a girl with bushy hair and a pale, round face. Thick eyebrows accentuated her well-defined almond eyes.

'Yes, that's correct,' he said, inadvertently using polite Japanese. Embarrassed at speaking so formally with a classmate, he rubbed his hand up and down the sleeve of his school uniform to cover up his confusion.

'Where're you from?'

'Minami-ku.'

'Oh, I used to live there. When I was in kindergarten.' Miyoshi narrowed her eyes and laughed in a low voice. Disconcerted at being talked to by a girl and yet pleased at being noticed, Izumi felt his body temperature rise.

Perhaps because the junior high school was in a new housing development where kids were more fashion conscious, most of the girls ignored the strict school dress code, wearing their skirts so short they exposed their knees. Many of them even plucked their eyebrows or dyed their hair a lighter shade of brown, but Miyoshi's hair was a jet-black bob, making her look like a Japanese doll. She wore her skirt down to her shins, which made her appear remarkably unsophisticated. But her innocence put Izumi at ease.

It was after the summer holidays that she transformed into what seemed a completely different person. When she entered the room on the first day of the autumn term, the entire class was stunned. Her hair was neatly combed and brighter in colour. Her hemline stopped above her knees, exposing the whiteness of her thighs, and her ample bosom pushed up her blouse. A closer look revealed a thin gloss of lipstick on her lips, and a sweet perfume rose from her neck.

'Miyoshi's making out with Mr Sakota.' Yamauchi, a member of the soccer team, whispered this to Izumi during lunch break. Rumours swept through the class. They'd been kissing in the classroom after school. They'd gone to a family restaurant together on Sunday. Someone had seen them coming out of a love hotel.

Everyone trained their curious eyes on the guileless Miyoshi. Sakota's classes tended to put everyone to sleep because he mumbled, but not today. When he took to the podium to teach maths, the students watched him and Miyoshi with bated breath.

After school that day, Izumi got on his bike and passed through the gate alone.

Someone shouted, 'Give me a lift, would you!' Miyoshi dashed up. It was the first time they'd spoken since before the summer break. 'We're going the same way,' she said, and, without giving him a chance to refuse, plonked herself onto the back of his bike, holding down her short skirt.

After-school clubs were already in session, so fortunately none of their classmates were around. What would they say if they saw this? Izumi pedalled vigorously to get away from the school before anyone discovered them. As the bike picked up speed, Miyoshi slipped her arms around his waist. Her soft bosom pressed against his back.

'Have you ever been in love, Izumi?'

'Huh? What's this about?' He feigned indifference, trying to mask his confusion. Bathed in the strong rays of the lingering summer sun, the pavement radiated a blistering heat. The weight of two people made pedalling hard work, and Izumi was soon out of breath.

'You haven't?' The sound of Miyoshi's low voice murmuring in his ear was strangely sensuous.

'There was a girl in elementary school I liked once.'

'What was she like?

'Kind of tall, and a really fast runner.'

'Are you serious? Those are usually things girls like. Was she cute?'

'Probably,' he answered. The face of his first crush, the tall, swift runner, was blurred. All he remembered was her silhouette. It looked beautiful when she ran.

'How 'bout you, Miyoshi? You in love with someone?' They had come to the bottom of the hill, and Izumi stood up on the pedals, hurling out this question with the same vigour as his pumping legs.

'You bet!' she shot back. An honest answer to his disingenuous question. 'And he's way older than me!' she added at the top of her lungs.

'Why him?' Caught off guard, Izumi's voice cracked.

'Well . . . Maybe because he's mature?' She said this almost as if she were asking herself a question. 'He's not really my type though. He's not good-looking, and he's more than twice my age. I started going out with him because he was so insistent, but . . .'

'Did you break up?'

'Nope. I ended up falling in love with him.'

'What's wrong with that?'

'It seems kind of unfair, right? I'm always the one who contacts him. I even write him letters. But he's grown so cold lately. Maybe he doesn't like me anymore.'

A moss-green cardigan that had seen better days. Clouded spectacles with tortoiseshell frames. Sakota, who always muttered the solution to a formula as he wrote it on the blackboard. What words would he use to respond to Miyoshi? Would he murmur in her ear 'I like you' or 'I love you'?

He felt a strange affinity with Miyoshi, a sentiment tinged by neither sympathy nor pity. 'He's probably busy.'

'Just as I thought. You've never been in love, Izumi.' The hill grew steeper, and the bike handles wobbled. He could feel Miyoshi's grip on his waist tighten. 'Cuz when you're in love, things like being busy or reserved just don't matter anymore.'

'Really? Is that what it's like?'

'Uh-huh. All you can think about is the other person. Falling in love makes people stupid.'

When they reached the top of the hill, Miyoshi jumped off the back of the bike. 'I'm going that way so I'll get off here.' The hem of her skirt flipped up. Before Izumi could catch his breath and ask if it was Sakota, she was racing towards the pedestrian crossing where the cutout-doll figure on the green walk light blinked impatiently.

'Izumi!' Miyoshi shouted from the other side of the crossing. He turned to look at her. In the slanting light, the trees cast long shadows over the road between them.

'Don't tell anyone! It's a secret!'

She gave a buoyant grin and waved. Her almond eyes looked like slender lines drawn across her fair-skinned face. Her husky voice was still the same as when he'd first met her, despite her sudden transformation. He burst into a grin and returned her wave. That was the last time he remembered talking with her.

Sakota's resignation was abrupt. It was rumoured that the teachers found out about their relationship, and, when pressed by the principal, Sakota confessed. Some of Miyoshi's classmates claimed excitedly that they'd seen her father march into the staffroom, looking livid.

On the day Sakota retired, the class wrote him a joint letter on a sheet of coloured paper. Among the many conventional messages that said things like, 'Thank you, Teacher. Take care of yourself,' there was one that stood out.

I wish I could forget you. But I'm sure I never will.

In contrast to the colourfully illustrated messages of the other girls, Miyoshi had written just these two lines and her name in black ballpoint pen. The spidery letters were scrawled in a corner of the sheet.

Izumi felt he could hear Miyoshi's low voice murmuring in his ear: Falling in love makes people stupid.

'Your mother called me last night. She said she wants to take a break from teaching for a while.' Miyoshi returned to the living room from the kitchen where she'd been making more tea. She placed a plate of assorted animal-shaped biscuits beside his cup. 'I'm afraid this is all we have,' she said. 'I was surprised. It seemed so sudden, you know. Is she okay?'

'Yeah. Sorry not to tell you sooner.'

ELEPHANT. HIPPO. COW. RABBIT. Izumi gazed absently at the animal silhouettes. Baked a light brown, the centre of each biscuit was branded with an English word.

'Miku really looked forward to her lessons, so she was kind of disappointed. She seemed so well though. Your mother, I mean.'

'Actually . . . That's why I came. I wanted to ask you about that.'

'About what?'

'My mother. I was wondering how she's been lately.'

He'd come without telling Yuriko. How far advanced were her symptoms? What should they do next? The night before he'd lain in bed researching dementia. Before he realised it, it was already dawn.

By the time he woke, it was early afternoon. He went down to the living room and found his mother sitting in front of the piano, gazing absently out the window. Soft spring sunlight bathed the garden. 'Poor Miku,' she said. She still seemed to be fretting about her piano lessons. That thought had made him wonder if perhaps Miku or her mother might have noticed any symptoms, and so he'd paid them a visit.

'I wonder. I didn't spend much time with her myself.'

Miyoshi looked uncertain, and Izumi pressed her further. 'Any little thing would help. If you noticed anything at all, please tell me.'

'She did seem to lose weight rather suddenly. She looked smaller somehow.' Miyoshi paused, then said, 'Why don't we ask Miku?'

She called her daughter, and the 'Turkish March' came to a halt. There was a pitter-patter of feet, and a little girl appeared. She looked identical to her mother, like a clone but half the size. Seeing the biscuits on the table, she asked if she could have some and picked up a penguin. She popped the penguin, followed by a camel, into her mouth before answering Izumi's question. 'She always makes a mistake at the same place,' she said.

'The same place?'

'The "Turkish March". She always makes a mistake in the same place I do.'

'I wonder why,' Izumi said with a laugh, and kept Miku company by eating a cookie stamped with the word BEAR. The pleasant aroma of butter along with a hint of sweetness spread through his mouth. 'That's odd for a teacher, isn't it?'

'That's right. She says, "Oops, I made a mistake. Sorry," then she plays it again, but makes the same mistake and stops.'

Miku popped one animal after another into her mouth. Was she worried about Yuriko? Or was she unconcerned? Izumi couldn't tell from her expression. Before he knew it, there was only one biscuit left on the dark blue plate. The golden-brown BAT seemed to stare up at him.

Orange sunlight poured into the entranceway through a round window above the front door. Miyoshi, who stood in the hall while Izumi was putting on his shoes, suddenly recalled something.

'Once, when I took Miku there, your mother rushed out of the house.'

'On the day of Miku's lesson?' Izumi asked as he stubbed his toes against the tiles, trying to get his trainers on. They were one size too small. A mistake he'd made when online shopping.

'That's right. I asked her where she was going, and she said she had to go and pick someone up. When I asked her who it was, she couldn't answer, so I told her it was Miku's lesson that day. She seemed to recollect herself then, and apologised, saying something about how she was getting forgetful. It seemed a little odd.'

'How long ago was that?'

'About three months ago. I'm sorry. I did think it was strange at the time, but after that she seemed perfectly normal. And she went on giving lessons the same as usual.'

'No need to apologise, Miyoshi. I didn't realise she wasn't well either.'

His right heel would not fit into his shoe, and he kicked his toe against the tiles repeatedly. With a noise like gravel scraping, the rubber covering the toe of his trainer peeled off. Izumi sighed. The brown adhesive showing through where the rubber had peeled back looked dirty.

'Izumi,' Miyoshi said as he stood gazing down at his shoe. 'Please tell her not to worry. And that I hope she'll teach Miku piano again when she can.'

Izumi went into the pharmacy in front of the station and was momentarily blinded by the harsh fluorescence. The PA system blared non-stop, announcing sales and special deals, and shop staff rushed about restocking shelves. He hadn't felt like going back to Yuriko's right away when he left Miyoshi's house, so instead he had walked fifteen minutes to the station.

If you need anything, I'll pick it up, he'd told Yuriko by phone, and she'd asked him to get some fabric softener and dish detergent. He put these items in the shopping basket and, returning to a stack of toilet rolls at the entrance, took a package. There was no toilet paper in the bathroom at Yuriko's; just a box of tissue on the floor. When he'd lived at home, she'd always made sure to buy extra dish detergent and toilet roll because she hated to run out.

On his way to the checkout counter, he passed an array of senior-care products. Things like adult nappies and incontinence pads, disposable waterproof sheets, oral care gel, high-calorie nutritional supplements and soft foods for ease of swallowing, such as ready-to-eat rice porridge in plastic pouches. He'd never noticed before how many home care goods there were in a pharmacy. This pharmacy, as well as the bus stop and the convenience store in front of the station, was full of seniors. What had once been a 'new town' had turned into an 'old-folks' town. The prophesy pronounced by the doctor loomed in front of him: a day will come when one in five seniors have dementia.

When Yuriko finished the package of assorted sushi Izumi had bought at the supermarket, she went into her bedroom without saying a word. Like a little girl who can't fight off sleep. It was still only nine at night. Izumi washed the dishes piled in the sink and scrubbed off the spills on the stove.

Almost all the things jammed into the refrigerator were past their best before date, and mould was growing in the hydrogen-water tank. Izumi emptied the fridge and threw everything into rubbish bags. He then cleaned the clogged drains in the bath and sink, which were matted with multiple layers of fine white hair. Had his mother done the same when he was a child, waiting to clean until after he'd dropped off to sleep?

As he was tidying a drawer overflowing with flyers and utility receipts in the dish cabinet in the dining area, he came across a stack of memoirs of people with dementia and books on treating it. He wondered when she had bought them. With a twinge of apprehension, he picked up one of the books and found an envelope tucked inside.

'Maybe she should come live with us,' Kaori said. She sat in front of him, gripping the sides of her tote bag. Her maternity tag swung from the handle.

'I don't think it would be so easy,' said Izumi, hanging on to the strap as he looked down at her. 'We're going to have a baby, and our apartment's too small.' The morning subway was crowded, and they spoke in low voices.

'I don't mind moving.'

'Think about it carefully. We're still paying our mortgage.' They had thirty years to go before they paid off the loan on the apartment in Shinjuku. 'We'll be raising a child, and you want to go back to work, right?'

'What about your mother? What does she want to do?'

'She wants to try living on her own for a while. She probably doesn't want to leave the place she's used to either.'

'Don't worry about me,' Yuriko had said the night before as she stood at the door. 'I'm still okay.' She nodded two or three times as though trying to convince herself.

'I'll come again next week. If anything happens, call me anytime.' Unable to even muster a smile, Izumi stepped outside and closed the door on his anxious-looking mother.

'Are you going to get a caregiver then?'

'It doesn't look like she needs one yet, but she probably will soon. I think we've no choice but to start off with getting her a helper or using day service.'

Yesterday he'd phoned the care manager introduced by the ward office support centre. From her voice, he guessed she was middle-aged. In a bright, cheerful tone, she'd explained all the services for people with dementia.

'You mean nursing-care service, right?' Kaori asked.

'Apparently a helper is someone who comes to the home to cook meals and help give her a bath. Day service is a facility that takes care of seniors during the day, giving them a meal, a bath and some rehab.'

'If that works out, it would be great, but . . .' As Kaori murmured this, the subway shot out into the open air. Below them spread a university sports field. Students wearing white uniforms were running about waving sticks with what looked like a little basket on the end.

'And the fees are quite reasonable. There's long-term care insurance too.'

Kaori had once told him that the sport was called lacrosse. She'd said it was very strenuous, but in the soft spring light, it looked strangely relaxed.

'What should we do when she can't live on her own anymore?' Kaori asked. 'There'll probably be times like before when she goes out and gets lost.'

'If it gets bad, we may have no choice but to put her in a home.'

'But they're all full and it's not easy to get a space, right? I heard one of my relatives has been waiting for ages.'

Kaori caressed her abdomen as though worrying about the future of their child. Lately, it's been kicking a lot, she'd told him, and he'd placed his hand on her belly. The force transmitted through his palm was far stronger than he'd expected.

'Getting dementia isn't the end of everything. Rather, it's what you do after the diagnosis that counts,' the care manager had told him over the phone. 'While the quality or amount of care she gets won't stop the disease, we still try to do as much as we can.' She said this as though trying to encourage him and followed up with an explanation of the care service assessment system and how to use long-term care insurance. It shouldn't have been that difficult, but most of what she said spilled out of his ears.

The photo shoot for the artist's CD jacket finished in the evening. Instead of going back to the office, Izumi dropped into the hair salon he frequented. He'd been so busy taking Yuriko to the doctor and trouble-shooting at work that he hadn't had a haircut for two or three months.

Once he was seated, the same stylist as always began combing his hair. 'It's got quite out of hand, hasn't it?' Dressed in a leopard-print shirt that clung to his thin frame, with bright red skinny trousers and thick-soled boots, he looked more like a punk rocker than a hairdresser.

'Yeah, it's a real drag having to tame it every morning.'

'If you don't take care of your appearance, you'll start ageing before you know it,' the stylist laughed, and the stud protruding from the side of his mouth jiggled. Although he looked intimidating, he always made Izumi feel at ease.

'You've got more grey already,' he added. Squeezing a lock of hair between his index and middle finger, he began to cut.

'I thought so,' Izumi said. Although he could have just talked to the stylist's reflection in the mirror, he couldn't help looking at him over his shoulder.

'It's particularly noticeable at the back.' The stylist gently turned Izumi's head forward and kept clipping away. One of the newer staff members who'd given Izumi a shampoo had told him this stylist was far superior to any of the others and would be made shop manager next year.

'If you're worried about it, you could dye it. Though I think it's got class like this too.'

As the words reached Izumi's ears, the pungent odour of hair dye pricked his nostrils. Beside him, a middle-aged woman was having her long hair coated with dye to cover the grey. Until that point, Izumi hadn't even noticed the smell.

Around the time he entered university, Yuriko had started buying hair dye. She'd stored it under the sink out of sight, perhaps feeling embarrassed. When he found the bottle hidden behind the stock of laundry detergent and shampoo, he'd realised for the first time that his mother was growing old.

The white envelope he'd found tucked inside a book about dementia in Yuriko's house last weekend bore the name of a general hospital located in the neighbouring district. After finding it, Izumi had pulled up a chair at his mother's dining table. Three empty vases lined the windowsill. He heard the ticking of the clock above his head and looked up to see that his mother had already been asleep for two hours. After staring at the envelope for some time, he drew out the piece of paper inside. It was folded in thirds.

Uneven blood flow detected in the frontal and parietal lobes. Decreased blood flow seen particularly in the temporal and occipital lobes.

The report diagnosed in detail the symptoms observed in each part of the brain. Izumi saw the words 'Suspected Alzheimer-type dementia, follow-up observation.' He looked at the date on the report. Six months earlier.

In retrospect, he recalled his mother phoning frequently around that period. When he'd asked why she called, her answers were sometimes vague. Sorry, Mum, I'm busy, he'd said each time, and hung up. He hadn't gone to visit either, even though she lived only an hour and a half away by train.

He followed the trail of memories while watching in the mirror as the stylist mixed dark brown dyes. His mother must have started having symptoms around then. Although she hadn't told him anything, she was asking for help. Yet he'd missed the signs. Or maybe he hadn't. Maybe he'd just pretended not to notice. When he thought of his mother going to the doctor's exam all by herself, his breath caught in his throat.

The dark brown dyes gradually turned white. Gazing at the substance being bleached of colour in the plastic cup, he thought, I'm going to grow old too.

In five months, their baby would be born.

That's how it worked. One life pushed into the world, another pushed out.

7

I jab the doorbell with my index finger again and again.

A shrill ring follows each press. Footsteps approach and stop at the door. Someone's holding their breath on the other side, peering through the peephole. One by one, large drops of rain strike the roof. The door stays closed. Balling my hand into a fist, I knock. *Bam, bam, bam.* Raindrops splash against the back of my hand. *Izumi! Are you there?* The lock clicks, then turns, and the brown door slowly opens. *What do you want?* I can't see her face. *Is my son Izumi there? Your son Izumi? He hasn't come home yet. It's starting to rain, and it's really cold. I thought maybe he got lost, although he's in elementary school already so he should know his way home. But I'm so worried, I can't just sit around and wait. I thought he might have come here. To play with Miura. You know Izumi and Miura are good friends. They often play together.* Miura's mother's face appears through the crack in the door. Her eyes bore into me. Why doesn't she answer?

I almost start shouting, but force myself not to. I sense someone walking around upstairs. I knew it! *He's here, isn't he?* Miura's mother looks away. She must be lying. *Izumi, you're upstairs aren't you!* Pushing the front door open, I step inside. *Hey! What do you think you're doing? Stop that!* Miura's mother grabs my arm. Her face is flat and featureless. *Let go!* I wrench my arm away and run up the stairs, not stopping to take my shoes off. *Izumi . . . Izumi . . . Izumi. I'm on my way. I'm coming to save you!* Oh . . . The helper, Mrs Nikaido, is here too. She always comes in without asking. I better hide my money and my bank books. I'm so hungry. I want to eat when I feel like it! I can take a bath by myself, you know! I'm not a child! I reach the top of the stairs and open the door in front of me. Miura is sitting at his desk, eating a bun. *Miura, have you seen Izumi?* He stares at me, his eyes wide with fright. He must be hiding something too. Just as I scream, *Where's Izumi?* the crumbs on the desk begin to shudder. They scurry in all directions over the desk like ants. *Stop that!* Miura's mother grabs my shoulder from behind. *Why are you hiding him? Why? Why're you doing this?* A sound like a monster roaring comes from outside. *Rrrrrooooooooohn.* Creaking and groaning, the house begins to shake. An enormous shadow passes by the second-floor window. I run over and look outside. Power lines whip wildly back and forth. Is Asaba all right? I race from the room and down the stairs. Bursting through the front door, I see house after house slide down the hill in the pouring rain. I run down the slope, but don't seem to be getting anywhere. Your mother hasn't remarried yet, has she, Izumi? Is she feeding you properly? It must be hard without a father, right? An apartment block drifts by. Through the square windows, I see shapes, people of all sizes, large and small. Their shadows whisper as they pass. Yuriko sure has some nerve to come back after what she did. Poor Izumi must have been so lonely. *That's not true! I . . . Izumi too . . . Surely Izumi!* I walk alone down the middle of the empty street. I walk and walk, but there're no people or cars. I don't even hear any birds. Where's Asaba? I look up. At the end of the straight road lies the sea. On its surface floats a white ship. The rain has stopped. No, it hasn't. Someone's holding an umbrella over my head. Asaba stands beside me. *Sorry, Yuriko. Were you waiting long?* He smiles down at me, an umbrella in one hand. *No, don't worry about it. I like watching the boats from here.* He nods silently and wraps an arm around my shoulder. I can't tell Izumi, but right now, I'm the happiest I've ever been. Tears well in my eyes. This is the happiest time of my life. The monster roars again. *Rrrrroooooooooohn.* The ship pitches, jostled by incoming waves. *Izumi! Where are you? Did you go home on your own?* Maybe he's lost. An explosion booms, and I look up. Fireworks burst in semicircles against the grey sky. One . . . Two . . . Three. The lower half of each circle is gone, as if wiped away by an eraser. Oh. I've got to hurry and find my boy. *I'm sorry, Asaba. I have to go to Izumi. Yuriko, wait.* Shaking off his sad voice, I jump onto the ship and climb down into the cabin, one step at a time. Izumi must be hungry. I better make him some sweet rolled omelette. And his favourite hayashi rice too. I'm so hungry. Where should I hide my bank books? *Miku, play those notes, do and fa, properly. I already told you! I can take a bath by myself! Where am I, by the way?* I open a door in front of me. Little desks and chairs. A big blackboard. Izumi raises his hand, stretching it high and straight, right up to his fingertips. Melos was furious. He decided he must get rid of the tyrannical king. Melos doesn't understand politics. He's a village shepherd who plays his wooden flute and frolics with the sheep.

⁂

A gust of wind caught Izumi's umbrella, turning it inside out.

He could feel the metal ribs writhe and bend as they deformed. The wind and rain picked up as dusk approached. He'd been walking around for two hours already, but there was still no sign of Yuriko. Rainwater flowed down the hill like a river, and his trainers were drenched. 'Mum!' No matter how many times he shouted, his voice was drowned out by the pounding rain.

The weather forecaster on the morning news had warned that a typhoon would land in the Kanto area late that night. 'Maybe I'll come home early,' Izumi had murmured.

Raising her face from her magazine, Kaori had said, 'Should I make something to eat at home then? What would you like?'

'Gyoza.'

'How about stuffing them together? It's been a while.'

'Good idea.'

He'd left the office in the evening and stopped by the supermarket. As he was putting a package of ground meat and some gyoza skins into his basket, his phone buzzed. The screen flashed 'Helper Nikaido'. He hesitated to answer it. Glancing outside, he could see the trees waving wildly. Nikaido always called when there was some issue with his mother. Yuriko won't get in the bath. It seems like she's been overeating lately. She keeps saying she has less money than before. These reports unnerved him, but Nikaido just laughed and kept telling him, 'It's okay.'

Izumi pressed his ear to the phone. On the other end, he heard Nikaido's voice. It shook with an urgency he'd never heard from her before.

'Mr Kasai, your mother's gone! She wasn't there when I came to the house. I've searched all over the neighbourhood, but I can't find her anywhere. I just contacted the police.'

Izumi couldn't help sighing.

'I'm so sorry,' Nikaido said, her voice barely audible. She must have been searching frantically. He knew it was unreasonable to blame her. Nikaido came to his mother's house three times a week to provide support. He couldn't expect her to keep an eye on Yuriko twenty-four seven.

He quickly returned the food items to the shelves and threw the empty shopping basket onto a stack on his way to the exit. But the basket tilted and ended up perched at an angle on top. He strode off anyway, but unable to leave it like that, turned back and shoved the basket into place.

On the train, the conductor announced that there were delays due to the heavy rain. It was almost rush hour, but the train was unusually empty. Rain fell in sheets that wavered like curtains with each gust of wind.

For the past two months, Kaori hadn't been feeling well, and Izumi had been taking care of the housework. He'd reorganised the apartment for the birth of the baby and bought things they would need, such as a baby bed and bedding. At work, the producer from the TV station was being uncooperative, making it hard to resolve the scheduling conflict for the tie-in. As usual, Osawa acted as though it wasn't his problem, so Izumi ended up taking the brunt of it. Just as he'd feared, Nagai's music video had overrun the budget, and other problems kept cropping up, like contract errors and a scandal involving one of their artists. Izumi frequently ended up going into the office on weekends as well and was only able to spend half a day a week with Yuriko.

When Izumi did manage to visit, she complained about the helper, as if she'd been waiting for the opportunity. 'Mrs Nikaido barges into my house without even saying hello. There's less money than there should be too. She might be taking it, you know.'

'There's no way she'd do that, Mum.'

'I've told her a million times I can take a bath by myself, but she won't listen. I'm not a child.'

When he lived at home, his mother had never complained. Even if she was dissatisfied with something, she seemed to consider it a virtue to swallow her grievances and stay silent. Now it was as if she couldn't hold them back.

'She never gets meals ready in time either. I get so hungry I end up buying something at the convenience store. It makes me wonder why we bother asking her to come.' As she rattled on, she downed one cream puff after another. Izumi had bought four, but she devoured them all in no time, even though she'd just eaten lunch. She used to eat so little, but now she was growing plump. The change shocked him. Were her innate desires only now manifesting themselves?

'I'm hungry. What shall we do for lunch, Izumi? Want me to make hayashi rice?'

'I'm fine, Mum.' He tried to smile as best he could. Last month, the gas company had called to say the gas had been left on. His mother had probably started cooking something and forgotten. Ever since, he'd kept the main valve turned off.

Izumi got off at the station nearest Yuriko's house. Nikaido was waiting for him at the ticket gate. Her small, round form was engulfed in rain gear. 'I'm so sorry,' she said, bowing deeply. Nikaido, who was normally such an optimist that it made Izumi worry, was trembling; Izumi felt the blood leave his face at the sight. 'I've been looking for her everywhere but I just can't find her,' she said. 'Do you have any idea where she might have gone?'

Izumi pondered her question but drew a blank. He knew there was no point in blindly heading off in this downpour, but he had to do something. He opened his umbrella and began running up the hill towards the house.

Two weeks ago, Yuriko had wandered off in the middle of the night and pounded on the door of a house about fifteen minutes' walk away. Fortunately, the person who lived there hadn't made a fuss, so it didn't become a big deal. But when his mother kept saying, 'I was looking for you!' after Izumi had rushed to the scene, he lost it and yelled at her to stop.

He took her hand, and together they walked the midnight city. She drew him along after her, saying, 'This way, Izumi.' From behind, her movements seemed frenetic, like a character in a silent film. She would forge ahead at great speed, then pause suddenly, confused about which corner to turn at. As if trying to cover up her embarrassment, she shot questions at him. 'How's work, Izumi?' 'Have you decided a name for the baby yet?' Her voice echoed loudly down the quiet street.

'Shhh. Mum, keep it down.' Hearing the reproof in his own voice, Izumi realised she embarrassed him.

When his mother was diagnosed, the doctor had told him, 'People with dementia don't intend to wander off. They always have some destination in mind or a reason they can't stay still. Some are trying to get back to where they were born, while others are running away from home. So please don't think such behaviour's strange.' Still, Izumi couldn't keep himself from scolding. Whether at the front door as she left for day service or in a restaurant or the train station, whenever she began talking loudly, he raised his voice and told her to behave. 'You're not a child, you know!' he would say. He didn't want his mother to behave like this.

'Mum!' Izumi shouted repeatedly from the entranceway, but there was no reply. It was pitch dark inside. As usual these days, shoes lay strewn about. He left his crumpled umbrella inside the front door and went into the living room, where he turned on the light. The house felt empty. The only bright spot in the room was the purple hydrangea he'd bought with Yuriko the weekend before.

His faint hope that she might have returned home had been dashed, and he sank into the sofa. Water dripped from his wet hair and plopped onto the wooden flooring. Powerful gusts shook the wood-framed house. Where on earth could she have gone? And in the middle of a typhoon! He tried to remember the things she'd said, as though reeling in her words.

Every time he visited, she seemed to have become even more forgetful. 'The speed with which it advances really depends on the person,' the doctor had told Izumi when he'd asked if such rapid memory loss was normal. 'At times it seems to progress incredibly fast, only to abruptly slow down. This may be particularly true for your mother,' he added. 'Because she's still quite young.'

For the past month, Izumi had come to her place after work whenever possible and stayed over. At night, she frequently wandered off. He would bring her home and change her into her pyjamas, while she cried and insisted this wasn't her house. 'I want to go home,' she'd say, and start putting on a dress. When he finally got her calmed down and into bed, she would wake in the middle of the night and start tidying.

One night, he was woken by a noise. He got up and found Yuriko huddled on the floor beside the toilet. Feeling something cold and wet on his toes, Izumi glanced down and saw a yellow liquid spreading across the floor. The colour was so vivid, like lemon syrup on shaved ice, it took him a moment to realise it was urine.

He stripped off her sopping pyjamas, led her to the bath and ran the shower over her. He wanted to avert his eyes from her naked body. She stood bolt upright, immobile, and he heard himself say sharply, 'You could at least wash yourself.' She reached for the bar of soap and picked it up slowly, staring at it vacantly. The hot water from the shower hit her shrunken back. 'I'm sorry,

Mum.' Izumi took the soap from her hand and, bowing his head, washed her.

She stepped out of the shower, and Izumi dried her with a towel, then gave her a pair of absorbent underwear and pyjamas to change into. But she seemed to have forgotten how to dress herself and repeatedly put them on and took them back off again. Maybe she was embarrassed, or perhaps just drowsy. She kept asking, 'Izumi, did you eat supper properly?'

After that incident, her dementia seemed to settle down a little. Nikaido hadn't called him for several days now, and he'd been looking forward to having dinner with Kaori at home for the first time in a while.

This was no time to sit around and do nothing, he thought. He threw on a plastic raincoat that was in the house and went outside. The wind was even stronger. The flowers in the garden of the apartment block next door were waving about so violently he thought they might rip from their stems. Water streamed past his feet, and, in moments, his shoes were soaked through to his socks.

Yuriko on New Year's Eve, swaying back and forth on the swing. The signs were evident even then. Why hadn't he taken her to the doctor right away? As he asked himself unanswerable questions, he reached the park, but there were only the empty swings swaying in the wind. An idea popped into his head, and he turned and began running towards Miyoshi's house.

Miku answered the door. When she saw Izumi, dripping wet, she called her mother. Miyoshi told him that she'd seen Yuriko walking down the hill early that afternoon. She'd told Miyoshi she was going to get Izumi. With a quick bow of thanks, Izumi rushed off. 'Want me to go look for her too?' he heard Miyoshi yell after him.

Should he go and check out the station, the supermarket and the flower shop again? But if she'd gone down the hill early in the afternoon, that would've been five hours ago. Dread pushed bile up his throat. He ran down the hill, taking care not to fall. All his weight rode on his heels, jolting his stomach. The pelting of the rain blended with the gasping of his breath inside his plastic hood like a musical ensemble. Mum, where are you? As he ran searching for his mother, he suddenly remembered feeling like this before – forlorn and helpless.

He'd often got lost as a child.

'When Izumi was going to nursery school, he used to get lost so easily,' his mother had told Kaori when they first met, as though she thought it was funny.

'Really? I don't remember that,' Izumi had protested, but his mother had shrugged as if to say, you really don't remember?

'You used to run off on the way back home,' she said. 'Or when I was shopping at the supermarket. You'd disappear the second I took my eyes off you.'

Kaori laughed, arching an eyebrow. 'That's hard to believe. I thought Izumi was the model child type, but it sounds like he was quite a handful.'

'It's not fair to talk about things that happened before I was old enough to have any common sense,' Izumi said with a sheepish grin. 'You can't expect a little kid to—'

'Yes, he was,' his mother said, cutting him off. 'He got lost the first time I took him to an amusement park, too. The minute we walked through the gate he was gone. I didn't find him until sunset. I think we were only able to buy a bag of sweets before it closed.'

As he ran through the pouring rain, Izumi recalled his mother at the amusement park gate, arms outstretched, tears welling in her eyes. He hadn't understood why she was crying. As he searched for his lost mother, he remembered something else.

I used to get lost on purpose. I wanted Mum to look for me and find me.

The phone clenched in his hand shuddered. With a rain-soaked finger, he pressed the button, praying it was good news.

The police had just called, Nikaido said on the other end of the line. 'They found her. At the elementary school.'

'Thank goodness.' Izumi's fatigue caught up with him and his legs stopped moving. 'But what was she doing there?' he asked automatically. Even at a time like this, he still sought a reason.

'Just come as soon as you can. Please. I'm heading there now.'

Nikaido hung up without waiting for a reply. There was a stern note in her voice so unlike her usual laid-back tone that it pulled him together. She knew better than Izumi what his mother needed most.

Someone from the school was waiting for him at the gate and led him through the dark corridors. Probably due to the approaching typhoon, there were no students or teachers around. He left his shoes at the entrance, and his wet socks left footprints as he walked along the polished linoleum floor.

They reached the third floor, and his guide slid back the door at the very end of the corridor. In a corner of the dimly lit room, Yuriko sat huddled on a small chair designed for elementary school students. Around her stood Nikaido and three policemen. She had a black pump on one foot and a light green sandal on the other. Apparently oblivious of her mismatched footwear, she gazed blankly out the window at the school ground below. It looked like the surface of the sea.

'Mum!' Izumi yelled as he burst into the room. Angry words rose to his lips, but he swallowed them at the sight of Nikaido's tear-filled eyes. She sat with an arm wrapped around his mother's shoulders. 'I was so worried,' he said.

His voice cracked. Perhaps from the joy and relief of finding his mother. Or maybe from the shock of seeing her looking like a stranger. She must have been walking in the rain for a long time. Her light dress had changed colour, and water still dripped from her hair. Nikaido's raincoat lay draped over her shoulders. She looked up at Izumi, her face pale.

'Izumi . . . Where were you? I was looking all over for you.'

'Mum . . .'

'I'm sorry, Izumi. It's all my fault. I can't do anything right.'

'That's not true, Mum.'

'But I'm glad I've finally found you. I was so worried, you see.'

She laughed as though relieved. In the same instant, tears fell from the corners of her eyes. Her face was that of his mother, arms outstretched to embrace him at the amusement park.

Nikaido, who had been watching this exchange between mother and son, gave Yuriko's shoulders a squeeze. 'Yuriko, isn't that wonderful! You've found him!' Nikaido's lips were white with cold, but they curved upward in a smile of relief.

'Yes, thanks to you . . .' Yuriko bowed deeply to Nikaido and the police officers. 'My son got lost, you see. It was getting dark and starting to rain. Izumi went off without his umbrella. I was so worried. I thought he might be sopping wet and freezing somewhere.'

'Well, it's all right now, isn't it, Yuriko! He's right here!' Nikaido had regained her cheery voice. It bounced around the quiet classroom. Yuriko blinked twice, rubbed the back of her hand across her eyes to wipe away her tears and gazed up at Izumi. In her other hand, she gripped two umbrellas.

'Izumi raises his hand so nicely in class. Stretching it straight up to the tips of his fingers. It makes the teacher want to call on him. He's great at reciting. He recited the story "Run, Melos" at Parents' Day. The mother beside me said Izumi was really good. I thought so too. My heart was bursting with pride and happiness. I wonder when Izumi became so good at reading. I was always working, so I never had the chance to teach him how to read or write.'

When his mother had come to observe his class on Parents' Day, Izumi kept turning round to look at her. He was so happy she'd come. She'd taken a whole day off work for it, and he'd practised reciting the story every day after school because he wanted to please her. When he finished reciting at Parents' Day, he sat down and turned to look at her. Applause filled the room, and his mother gave him a little wave, her eyes moist. The Yuriko who sat before him now was gazing at him just like then.

8

Kaori pressed the white switch; the motor whirred to life with a dull hum. After a pause, water began trickling down a green plastic chute designed to look like split bamboo.

'Here it comes!' she said, following the water as it slid down the shallow slope of the *nagashi-sōmen* machine. Her eyes were sparkling as though watching an experiment.

Maki was seated beside Kaori at the dining table. 'Isn't it ready yet, Taro?' she called out.

Her partner, Taro, was battling with a large pot in the open kitchen. 'Almost!' they heard him shout, his face lost behind a cloud of steam.

'Sorry to take so long,' Maki said. 'You must be starving.' She stroked her belly as she looked at Izumi. Her abdomen was about the same size as Kaori's, their due dates about two weeks apart. Two women in their last month of pregnancy sitting side by side. They looked like twins out of some fairytale.

Before Izumi could respond, Kaori jumped in. 'Not at all. I should be the one apologising. For suddenly saying I wanted *sōmen*.'

'Is this your first time?' Maki asked.

'To use one of these machines? Yeah. I've always wanted to try one.'

Steam billowed up from the sink as Taro emptied hot water into it. A loud bang of rebounding stainless steel overlapped his exclamation of 'Ow, that's hot!'

'Here. Let me give you a hand,' Izumi said as he hurried into the kitchen. He steadied the pot, then quickly rinsed the noodles in a colander under cold running water.

'You seem to know what you're doing, Izumi,' Taro said.

'Cooking *sōmen* was always my job at home.' Izumi flicked the colander up and down, slapping the chilled noodles against the bottom to get rid of excess water.

Kaori and Maki had entered the company at the same time. While Kaori had rushed around the city as the new publicist, Maki, who'd grown up overseas and spoke fluent English, had been put in charge of Western pop music, organising big rock festivals and other events.

Maki spoke her mind in a way only someone who'd grown up overseas could; consequently, she didn't fit in at the office. Kaori had been uncomfortable with her at first too, but after transferring to the classical music department, she and Maki travelled overseas together on business trips. They both liked craft beer and wine, and, during one of those trips, they had bonded over a few drinks.

Kaori clapped her hands as Izumi placed a bamboo basket heaped with gleaming noodles on the table. 'Wow! Those look fantastic.'

Maki poured dipping sauce into small bowls. 'On with it!' she said. 'Let's get those noodles flowing.'

'How does it work?' Izumi asked, perplexed. Taro, who'd sat down beside him, grabbed a clump of noodles with his chopsticks and dropped them into the chute at the top of the machine. The noodles separated and slid down the slope, which was curved like a water slide.

'Here they come!' Maki stuck her chopsticks into the chute. The noodles wrapped around them, and she scooped them up and dunked them in the sauce, then ate them with a loud slurp. 'Your turn. Go for it!'

At her urging, Izumi grabbed a clump of noodles with his chopsticks. 'Get ready, Kaori!' he said, and dropped them at the top of the stream.

Following Maki's example, Kaori stuck her chopsticks into the chute and tried to catch the noodles, but they slipped between her sticks and landed in the basin at the bottom. Her eyes widened. 'That's surprisingly hard.'

'The trick is to scoop them up from underneath instead of trying to grab them between your chopsticks,' Maki advised. Kaori readied her chopsticks again. This time she stuck them beneath the sliding mass and raised them up, catching the noodles. They trembled on the end of her chopsticks, and she shouted with glee.

'Go on, eat!' Maki insisted, and Kaori slurped them down.

Maki grinned. 'Good, huh?'

'Even better than regular *sōmen*!' Kaori beamed as she downed another mouthful.

At the end of the previous year, Maki had told them she was getting married. Her partner was a publicist for an animation label; they'd met at the foreign record company Maki now worked for, having been headhunted away from Kaori and Izumi's company. After telling them she was engaged, she added that she was pregnant. It was so like her to announce the fact as casually as if it was a dessert that came with the meal.

Her partner, Taro, was an anime *otaku* who always wore a dungaree shirt with worn-out jeans and a sports-brand knapsack, while Maki dressed in primary colours and clothes that showed off her figure. When side by side, they didn't look like a couple, yet strangely enough, they got along well. 'For some reason, I feel comfortable when I'm with him,' Maki had said. Her face shone with happiness.

'How much weight have you gained?' Maki asked, dropping some finely chopped *myōga* ginger into her dipping sauce. Beside her, Taro was busy launching noodles down the chute.

'Nine kilos. It's getting bad. My doctor keeps warning me not to get any fatter.' Kaori said this as she grabbed another clump of noodles. 'I get it, you know, but I just can't seem to stop myself.'

'I've been walking down along the river every morning. We'll need to be strong to give birth.'

'I may be in trouble then. I'm getting hardly any exercise. Too busy at work.'

'Kaori, you're amazing, you know. I never work overtime. And I never hesitate to take a paid holiday.'

Izumi recalled that Maki had passed on most of her work to a junior colleague when she reached her second trimester. Because, she said, she wanted to enjoy her pregnancy. She'd always been the type to revel in new experiences and rarely went to the same restaurant or visited the same destination twice.

'Have you guys bought a pushchair yet?' she asked.

'Not yet,' Kaori said. 'Do you have any recommendations?'

'I think Japanese brands are best. Foreign-made pushchairs are too bulky. They won't fit through the ticket gates at train stations.'

'That makes sense. I'd better do my research.'

'How about a baby bouncer?'

'You think it's good to get one?'

'A must. Just being put in one seems to make babies stop crying. And I've read that cots with adjustable sides are much easier too.'

'Babies are surprisingly heavy, aren't they?'

'We're going to use the Gina method, so we want to be able to put the baby down gently.'

'Gina? What's that?' Kaori asked, her chopsticks finally pausing. Before they knew it, the bamboo basket was empty.

Taro went into the kitchen to boil some more noodles, and Izumi scooped up the stray strands still swimming about in the pool at the bottom of the chute.

'It's a child-rearing method developed by a charismatic nanny from England.'

'Sounds good, doesn't it, Izumi?'

'Yeah. Should we try it?'

That's right, he thought. We're going to be a normal mum and dad. Proud and confident. But this conversation right now made him feel uneasy, like they were just playing house.

When the two couples had realised they were expecting babies around the same time, they'd started getting together for meals. Whenever they met, Maki shared whatever she'd learned about birthing and child-rearing. And each time, Izumi and Kaori became acutely aware of how unprepared they were. Overwhelmed with work and caring for Izumi's mother, however, they had no time for anything else. Instead, they just kept accumulating information.

As if inviting Izumi, who'd been listening silently, to join the conversation, Maki turned to him and said, 'Kaori was seriously scary when I worked with her.'

Kaori's brow furrowed. 'Scary? I am not. Right, Izumi?'

'Hmm, let me see. No, I don't remember you coming across like that when I worked with you.' As he gave this noncommittal answer, his eyes shifted to the window behind her. Maki and Taro's apartment was on the upper floor of a high-rise in the Shitamachi area. In the distance, the buildings of central Tokyo shimmered in the midsummer sun like a heat haze. 'It's strange,' Kaori had told him on their way to Maki's, 'but pregnant women can talk about anything together.'

'You're sort of a perfectionist, you know, Kaori,' Maki went on. 'And because you expect that of others, your junior staff sometimes seemed a little overwhelmed.'

Izumi concurred with this allegation. 'People have said you're not the type to entrust things to others.'

Kaori laughed. 'Well, I can't argue with that.' She picked up her glass, which dripped with condensation, and downed the iced barley tea in one gulp. 'Guess that's why I still have so much work left to do.'

'You're incredible. I don't think I'll be able to go back to working the way I used to.'

Bang! The pop of the steel sink announced that the next batch of noodles was cooked. Before Izumi could get up, Taro announced feebly through a cloud of steam, 'It's okay, I think I can do it myself this time.'

'You say that,' Kaori said, 'but I bet you'll be back at work in no time, Maki.'

'I wonder. The only thing I was good at was speaking English. It wasn't like I was any good at my job. I think my boss knew that. That's why I switched to another workplace. I thought having a child would give me a chance to rethink work too. I'm not sure I can devote the same amount of passion to it anymore.'

Maki surveyed the room. Boxes of nappies, wipes and baby toys were stacked in a corner of the white-walled living room. She laughed as if to pull herself together. 'Kaori,' she said, 'you'll probably seek the same level of perfection in child-rearing as you do in your work.'

Izumi followed suit, hoping to lighten the mood. 'True, I can't imagine you letting things slide.'

'You might turn out to be pretty particular yourself, Izumi,' Kaori retorted, casting him a playful glare just as Taro brought over another basket of noodles. A few pink and pale green noodles peeked out of the white mass.

Izumi had often eaten *sōmen* noodles in summer as a child. He would boil them while his mother made sweet potato tempura. When they sat down at the table, Izumi would pick out the coloured noodles, while his mother stuck to the white ones.

As Izumi gazed at the noodles, Taro piped up from beside him. 'In the old days, those coloured ones were the best, weren't they?' Izumi didn't know how to respond, feeling as if Taro had read his mind. 'But somewhere along the way,' Taro continued, 'the regular old white ones got better.'

'Do you remember when that was, Taro?'

'Let me see . . . Nope. Can't remember at all.' He opened a bottle with an illustration of a bonito on it and topped up the sauce in his bowl.

'Is it a boy?' Kaori asked.

'No, a girl!' said Maki.

'Have you picked a name yet?'

'Nope. Haven't even started. Did you get the number of strokes in the characters evaluated?'

'I wonder if we should.'

'Taro and I went to a childcare class together.'

'Really? What was it like?'

'Kind of embarrassing. It made me feel awkward.'

'Are you listening to classical music as part of pre natal care?'

'I've been listening to things like Mozart, but I don't really get the point, you know.'

Izumi absently observed the two women's lively exchange, thinking all the while of his mother. It seemed to him she'd decided, from that day, to live a normal life. He was sure she'd consciously placed her son at the centre of her existence. But now that she had dementia, he felt he was being rejected by her all over again.

Kaori and Maki, and beside him, Taro, were slurping up noodles. They didn't bother to slide them down the chute anymore, taking them straight from the basket instead. The whine of the motor echoed through the dining room, and a lone pink noodle swam round and round the basin.

Vivid yellow flowers were prominently displayed in the shop in front of the station.

'They've got sunflowers already,' Kaori said, picking out three.

'Just one. It's a rule at our house,' Izumi said, returning two of them to the bucket.

Yuriko liked single-flower vases. It's wonderful how just one flower conveys the season, she would say every time they bought one together. Even if she got a bouquet at a wedding or some other occasion, she would pick out one flower and put it in a vase.

With the sunflower clutched in one hand, Izumi walked up the hill. Beside him walked Kaori. Her belly looked huge, and she wiped the sweat that sprang to her brow repeatedly. Izumi had suggested catching a cab from the station, but she'd chosen to walk because the doctor had advised her to get more exercise.

On the day Yuriko had been found in the classroom, she developed a high fever. It hadn't come down the next day, and she had a hacking cough along with it, so Izumi had called an ambulance. She was diagnosed with pneumonia and, at one point, her condition became so severe she lost consciousness. Izumi took an early summer holiday and commuted to the hospital to care for her. About a week after she was hospitalised, she recovered and was allowed to go home. The experienced nurse who had been primarily responsible for his mother's care patted Izumi on the shoulder when they left and said, 'I'm sure your mother recovered because you were here.'

In consultation with the doctor, it was decided that Yuriko could return home if she continued to receive support from a home helper and day service. Ever since Yuriko had begun wandering off, Kaori had been worried about her, but Izumi hadn't shared much about her condition. She'd be giving birth soon, and he didn't want to burden her with any extra stress. But when she heard his mother was to be discharged, Kaori said she wanted to see her, and they decided to go and celebrate her recovery.

'We're here,' Izumi called out as he opened the door, and Yuriko appeared from the far end of the corridor. The colour of her complexion was much better. She looked alert too, gazing straight at them, and Izumi felt a wave of relief.

'Come on in!' Noticing Kaori, she beckoned to her. 'Thank you for coming all this way. Come inside. Oh, look at you! You've grown so big.'

'Yes, and so heavy, it's hard to move.' Kaori walked into the living room, cradling her swollen belly in both hands.

'I know what you mean. When I was pregnant with Izumi, I gained so much weight, it was really hard. I drank Coke all the time, and the doctor scolded me.'

'For me, it was chocolate. I couldn't stop.'

'Really Miku? You too?'

'When I finally got over my chocolate craving, all I could eat was fried chicken.'

Yuriko laughed and flapped her hand as if to say, 'No worries.' 'You should eat what you like,' she said. 'Come now, Miku; have a seat on the sofa.'

'Mum.'

'What is it, Izumi?'

'This is Kaori. Not Miku.'

'Oh, did I make a mistake?'

'Uh-huh.'

'We brought some cake.' Kaori lifted the bag from the bakery, changing the subject. 'Why don't we have some together?'

'Yes, let's. I'll make tea. Or would you prefer coffee? I only have instant. Oh look, the flower has wilted. I better go buy a new one!' Yuriko took off her apron and started getting ready to go out.

'It's okay, Mum. We bought one at the station.' Izumi pointed to the flower he had laid on the dining table.

'Why thank you! A beautiful sunflower. Nikaido keeps catching colds, you see.'

'Catching colds?'

'Uh . . . I'm sorry. The doctor says I should exercise more often. But I get tired so quickly!' Yuriko put her hand over her mouth and doubled over laughing. She laughed so long and hard her shoulders shook.

'Mum, get a grip on yourself.' Although Izumi smiled along with her, cold sweat dripped down his back. Kaori was smiling too, but her hands clutched her swollen belly.

'Oh dear, I'm getting so muddle-brained,' Yuriko muttered, suddenly serious. She opened the dish cupboard and reached for a dish in the back but seemed to have trouble extracting it. The clatter of dishes jostling against each other broke the silence.

'You're doing fine, Mum,' Izumi said. He couldn't stand to watch her struggling anymore and reached out a hand to help.

'Don't treat me like an idiot!' his mother shrieked. She grabbed a random assortment of bowls and small plates, as many as she could carry in both hands, and ambled towards the kitchen. One by one, they began slipping from her grasp to the floor, rolling across it with a dull sound.

'I don't want to go!'

'Mum, calm down.'

'You're going to leave me because I left you, aren't you?'

Kaori clung to Izumi's arm. The sight of Yuriko so distraught had robbed her of words.

'I'm sorry Izumi,' his mother pleaded. 'I promise I won't leave you again. I'll do everything right. I'll do the laundry and the cleaning. I can cook properly too.' Still clutching dishes in her hands, she went into the kitchen.

'Your favourite. Miso soup with turnip. I made a big pot of it just now.'

Miso soup? Izumi cocked his head. The gas was turned off when his mother was on her own. How could she have made miso soup? He followed her into the kitchen and lifted the lid off the pot on the burner.

Condominiums. Unwanted Articles Pickup Service. Just 198 Yen. New Pachinko Machines. Recruiting Part-Time Workers.

Sentence fragments printed in colourful letters greeted his eyes. Strips of paper cut from fliers floated in the water filling the pot. Izumi couldn't breathe. He slammed the lid back down. His eyes met Kaori's where she had sunk back onto the sofa. She seemed to have guessed it wasn't soup in the pot.

'We should eat it while it's hot.' His mother, who had moved soundlessly to his side, opened the freezer and took out a pair of frost-covered chopsticks. They rattled. She walked over to the stove, lifted the lid and stared at the 'miso soup'.

'Izumi . . . I'm sorry I left you . . . You must have been so lonely.'

'It's all right, Mum.'

'From here on, I'll be with you every day. I'll stay with you forever, so please . . . forgive me.'

Yuriko picked up a ladle and began stirring the contents of the pot. The wet strips melted into the water and swam around in circles like fish.

Izumi smelled the aroma of miso soup.

Even though it should have been odourless, the smell penetrated his nostrils, convulsing his stomach. Overcome with an urge to vomit, he pressed both hands against his mouth.

'Izumi, are you okay?' He heard Kaori's voice from behind. In front of him, his mother kept stirring the pot. The same way she had that time. *Mum, stop! Please!* He couldn't keep himself from gagging. With his hands still pressed over his mouth, he ran to the toilet and heaved. Whatever had been building up inside him for so many years now spewed from his mouth and ran down the inside of the white porcelain bowl.

9

Izumi waded through the noise of the cicadas and dashed inside the automatic doors.

He'd only walked about five minutes from the subway station, but already his shirt was sticking to his sweat-drenched back. The cicadas' roar was replaced by the uniform sound of a Vocaloid overlapped with punk-rock guitar. Music videos by artists currently promoted by the label were being played on three monitors on the wall in front of Izumi.

A trio of women manned the reception desk beside the monitors. Like the 'twin' receptionists at Izumi's office, they looked identical. As soon as his gaze met theirs, however, they bowed and smiled. Accustomed to receptionists who never looked up from their computers, let alone greeted him, Izumi hastily averted his eyes. If reception was so different within the same record industry, he wondered somewhat anxiously what kind of impression his company made on visitors.

He and Nagai were meeting a representative of a different label to discuss a tie-in with one of its vocal units. It was time for their appointment, but Nagai had yet to turn up. A receptionist led Izumi to the café space on the second floor, explaining that the representative was in another meeting and running late.

The broad window looked out on a grove of trees, deep green and probably teeming with the cicadas that were even now hurling noise towards the building. The waitress handed him a menu that featured a photo of colourful tropical juice. It seemed to be the monthly special. Izumi wondered who would order such a fancy-looking drink. He stared at the photo, tempted to try it himself, but was caught off guard by the voice of the waitress asking him what he'd like. He ordered something less adventurous instead.

Putting the straw to his lips a little while later, Izumi sucked up iced coffee. Before he knew it, half the brown liquid in the plastic cup was gone. He paused and took a deep breath. He'd finally stopped sweating. The café space that evening was crowded with employees, name cards dangling from their necks as they tapped at their laptops or talked business with clients. Izumi glanced at the entrance and saw Nagai searching for him; Izumi waved. Nagai stopped to order something, then continued towards him, raising one hand in front of his face as though in supplication. 'Sorry to be late,' he said.

'I saw it streaming in Shibuya,' said Izumi. 'Very impressive.'

'What?' asked Nagai. As he sat down, the waitress placed a mug of coffee gingerly in front of him. It looked like it might overflow at any moment. Izumi slurped up the remains of his iced coffee.

'Ongaku's new music video of course,' he said.

'When you consider how much it cost, it kind of sticks out like a sore thumb, doesn't it?'

'Don't you go saying that.' With a wry smile, Izumi gave Nagai's baseball cap a playful whack, dropping the visor down over his eyes. Beneath it, he could see Nagai's lips curve into a grin as he mouthed, 'Sorry.'

Just two days before the shoot, Izumi had discovered that production costs were almost double the budgeted amount. He'd had a bad feeling about it from the very beginning and had kept asking Nagai to fill him in on progress. But each time, Nagai said he was currently negotiating costs and that the director had assured him there'd be no overrun. The truth finally came out when the production company called Izumi to beg for his help because they couldn't possibly keep costs within the budget.

Infuriated by this unprecedented overrun, Osawa ordered Izumi to halt production immediately. 'Who's going to take responsibility?' he yelled, from which Izumi gathered it wouldn't be Osawa. Yuriko had begun wandering off around this time, and it would have made Izumi's life a lot easier to call off the project, but he went ahead with it anyway. The content of Nagai's proposal had more impact than anything he'd seen in a long time, and Izumi had learned when he started at the label that hits are only born from what seem like the craziest ideas.

After persuading Osawa to continue on condition that they slashed projected costs by thirty per cent, Izumi had worked with the production company to whittle down expenses. He and Nagai both had to submit written apologies for poor project management, but the resultant music video was a masterpiece of fantasy that showcased the director's genius at its best, visually capturing the band's ethos. A special set was erected in the studio to recreate Shibuya's Scramble Crossing as Ongaku's stage. As the music poured from their instruments, gusts of wind, flashes of lightning and huge waves crashed down upon the city. The bizarre video became an internet sensation, chalking up more than a million views in the first three days and catapulting Ongaku to fame.

'How many views so far? On YouTube I mean.'

'Over five million when I checked this morning.'

'Amazing.'

'Yeah, but Tanabe's furious. She jumped on Osawa this morning, demanding to know if he thinks the end justifies the means. What a drag.' But his mouth twitched as he said this, and he didn't look the least bit bothered as he drew his phone from the pocket of his hoodie and gazed at the bluish glow of the screen.

'What did Osawa say?' Izumi asked.

'He said, "It's fine. So long as it all works out."'

'Sounds just like him.'

'Yeah. But that made Tanabe even madder. They argued pretty spectacularly for a while. Still flirting like always. They get along so well.'

Although Nagai sounded cheeky, Izumi didn't mind his choice of words. He felt Nagai was saying the things he wanted to say himself but couldn't.

'They're still together, huh?'

'It'd be a real headache if they decided to break up, so I hope they make it work.'

'Good point. And what about your next video? Are you going to use the same director?'

'Nah. I think I'll pass on working with a genius again. Too exhausting. Once was enough. What about you? You look tired.'

Izumi was about to retort that this was partly Nagai's fault, but checked himself when he saw Nagai's serious expression. His deep-set, double-lidded eyes peered out from under the visor of his cap.

'Is everything okay? With your mother?'

Izumi had told his co-workers about Yuriko's condition – that he might have to take a few days off or leave early depending on how she was doing. When she had been hospitalised with pneumonia, he'd explained the situation and taken time off. Unlike Tanabe, who'd offered words of sympathy, Nagai had looked indifferent and said nothing, but for Izumi, that was easier.

'What's with this sudden interest?' Izumi said. It probably wasn't the right thing to say to someone expressing concern about his mother, he thought, but he couldn't respond like usual when Nagai was so unexpectedly serious.

'Well, actually, we had a pretty rough time with my grandmother when she went senile,' Nagai said. 'She was really fond of me when I was little, but once I started working, I fell out of touch. By the time I went to see her, her dementia was quite advanced.'

'Alzheimer's?'

'Frontotemporal. She found it hard to accept a helper coming in and was verbally abusive. She also overate and wandered off a lot. Your wife works too, so I just wondered if you guys were doing okay.'

The buzzing of the cicadas reached Izumi's ears again, and he glanced around the café. It had been full when he came in, but now it was almost empty.

'My mother left home once.'

Izumi had told Kaori this while they lay in bed after returning from their visit to Yuriko's place.

'When I was around thirteen.' He guessed Kaori was asleep, but he kept talking anyway. 'For about a year.'

The light of a street lamp slipped through a crack in the blackout curtains, drawing a pale line on the bedroom ceiling.

He heard Kaori's voice beside him.

'I figured something like that might've happened. Your relationship with Yuriko is a little odd, you know.'

'Odd?'

'Uh-huh. Quite strange really. It's hard to tell if you're close or distant.'

'I see. I wonder which.'

He was surprised that she'd guessed, but also relieved. I really am oblivious, he thought. I'm always the last one to notice these things.

'I can sort of understand how Yuriko might have felt,' Kaori mused. 'If she raised you all on her own, she must have longed to escape sometimes. Even I get anxious when I think about the future.'

Her voice seemed to be directed at the pale line on the ceiling. A motorbike revved outside the window, and a milky-white light moved across the line.

'So, what're you going to do about your mother?'

Nagai's voice, slightly raised, pulled Izumi back to the present. He sighed. 'I can't take much more time off, and we'll be having a baby soon.' He sipped the melted ice at the bottom of the plastic cup through the straw. Mixed with the remains of the coffee, the pale brown liquid tasted faintly of chlorine.

'It's hard to find a good nursing home these days too, isn't it? My grandma had to wait a long time to get in. And as soon as she did, she got pneumonia and died. How 'bout you guys?'

'Actually, we got a space in one just yesterday.'

'Seriously?' Nagai yelped. 'How'd you manage that?' He brought the rim of the brimming cup cautiously to his lips.

'I guess we were just lucky.'

The day before, Izumi had received a call from the director of the facility where he'd put his mother on the waiting list. 'Mr Kasai,' the woman had said. 'A space has opened up.' Before the stunned Izumi could respond, she asked, 'When do you think you can move in?'

Izumi and Kaori had decided to put Yuriko in a nursing home after the 'miso soup' incident at her house. Until then, Kaori had still seemed to think that living together might be a possibility, but once she saw Yuriko's behaviour, she agreed with Izumi. After consulting a friend with experience in geriatric care, she realised how difficult it would be to balance caring for both a newborn and her mother-in-law.

On weekends, they visited different nursing homes near Yuriko's house, but none of them seemed likely to suit her. When Izumi confided this to Nikaido, she told him she knew a good place and introduced them to a group home located by the sea. 'It's small, run by a mother and her daughter,' Nikaido had said. 'But their approach is quite unique, and the place is highly recommended. It's got a great view too, because it's right by the shore.'

Izumi took the train to the nearest station, a twenty-minute ride. From there, it was ten minutes by taxi. The group home, a large, renovated old house, came into view as the taxi rounded a corner. He was met at the entrance by the director, a short, middle-aged woman with a childlike face, and her daughter, who looked just like her but was a head taller. 'Welcome to Nagisa Home. I'm Mizuki, the director,' the middle-aged woman said, smiling as she led Izumi inside.

Izumi rapidly explained that his mother had dementia and had begun wandering; that his work in Tokyo kept him busy and that his wife was expecting a baby; that they had looked at several facilities, but hadn't wanted to put his mother in any of them. All the while, Mizuki and her daughter sat on the sofa across from him, their heads inclined as they listened. Probably his story was not uncommon. Their eyes seemed to say, 'It's all right.' Occasionally, a man with a cane wandered in front of Izumi, and a woman with a humped back came and sat between the director and her daughter, but they seemed unperturbed.

'Mr Kasai,' Mizuki said. 'Do you ever go to a McDonald's or a Doutor Coffee shop?'

'Yes,' he answered in a small voice, wondering where this question was leading.

'Would you spend seven or eight hours there?'

'No, I don't think I'd last that long.'

'That's right. It's hard even for healthy people to stay in one place too long.'

In the garden outside the window, a chihuahua yawned as it basked in the warm sun. Mizuki had told Izumi it had belonged to a resident who'd moved in last year but had died. She and her daughter had kept the chihuahua, and now all the residents took care of it. She'd concluded with a rueful shrug that the dog was getting quite fat because they fed it too much.

'Linoleum floors. White concrete walls. Everyone watching one little TV and eating from plastic dishes.'

'Er, yes?'

'If you had to live in a place like that, how many days do you think you'd survive?'

'Uhm . . . I wonder.'

'Every facility has its own approach, and, of course, there are costs and efficiency to consider, but personally, I don't think I could stand such a place for even half a day. I'd be dying to run away. How can we imagine that people with dementia would want to live in such places if even their family members can't wait to get away when they visit? No wonder residents try to escape. Facilities add more doors to keep them in, but that just makes them more anxious to get out. Some may become verbally abusive or even violent, but I think that's a pretty normal response.'

'Does everyone here have dementia?'

The residents sitting around the dining table de-stringing string beans and chatting about what to make for supper didn't look like people suffering from some form of brain disease. A woman in a rocking chair by the window was deftly knitting lace on a pair of needles.

'Yes, all of them. They may no longer remember the meaning of words or events, but they do retain their memory of how to do things. That's why they can still cook or do crafts, even though they can't remember names.

We try to avoid exposing them to cold, inorganic stimuli by using materials like wood or cloth, so that everything they see or touch feels natural. Although we never lock the doors and windows, almost no one runs away. Wandering and aggressive behaviour are just symptoms. Dementia may be impossible to cure, but we believe such symptoms can be suppressed by reducing stressors.'

Izumi's gaze was drawn to a black upright piano in a corner of the room. It was old but well cared for. He stared at it for a long time, and Mizuki's daughter, who'd been listening silently, now spoke up. 'One of the residents brought it with her. Her family let us keep it when she passed away.'

The sight of the piano gleaming in the white sunshine made Izumi feel for the first time that he'd found the right place for his mother. It seemed fitting that she should have music in her final home. He was also sure that this was the kind of place anyone would want to live. 'How long will we have to wait before she can move in?' he asked, suddenly anxious.

'All of our residents have lived here a long time. Some more than ten years. We've got a long waiting list. There're a few people who've been on it for over five years.'

Although he knew this was only to be expected, Mizuki's words plunged Izumi into despair. His mother couldn't wait five years. They'd have to look elsewhere. He asked them to add his name at the bottom of their long list, feeling as if he was betting on the lottery.

So when the director called, he wondered what miracle had occurred. She told him that three residents who'd lived at Nagisa for many years had passed away around the same time. When she'd contacted the people on the list in order of their applications, many had either already died or found another place.

Izumi promised to move Yuriko in at the beginning of the following month and then immediately called Nikaido. They'd moved from the end of the line to the front in a single bound.

'That's great, Izumi,' Nagai murmured while fiddling with his phone, perhaps replying to a text. His thumb flicked back and forth over the screen.

'Bet you don't mean that.'

'Course I do,' Nagai answered, his eyes still fixed on the screen. Izumi had realised about half a year ago that when Nagai wanted to talk about what was really on his mind, he would speak while looking at his phone or computer.

'I mean it. Seriously, I'll do my best to fill in for you.'

'Good. I'm counting on you,' Izumi said just as one of the receptionists came and called their names. Their scheduled appointment should have started twenty minutes ago. 'Finally,' Izumi muttered. He rose to his feet with a sigh.

'Izumi.'

Izumi turned at the sound of his name and saw Nagai, cap in hand, looking straight at him.

'I've been meaning to say this for a long time.'

'Say what?'

'I'm sorry for all the trouble I caused with the Ongaku video. The production costs. I knew from the start we couldn't possibly stay within the budget, but I went ahead anyway. I was prepared to be fired for it, if it came to that.'

Nagai bent at the waist, bowing deeply. Steam still rose in a thin thread from the coffee cup on the table in front of him.

'I thought if I just did what I was told and produced safe, mediocre work I'd never be recognised as anything. I'm no good at talking, and I suck at socialising and organising. So, I figured I'd have to make up for it in production . . . and I got reckless.'

As Izumi stood stunned, not knowing how to reply, vivid gradations of red and orange passed in front of him. Four female employees clutched glasses of tropical fruit juice the colours of a sunset sky, each one topped with a large chunk of pineapple and a scarlet cherry.

'Izumi, thanks for letting me make that video. I'll try not to cause any more trouble and do my best to take some of the load off you. I feel a lot of regret about my grandmother. She lost her memory so fast and forgot who I was. She died before I had a chance to get to know her. So please, use this time for your mother.'

10

The summer sun struck the water's surface, creating a pathway of light.

'Look. The sea,' Izumi said to Yuriko as he rolled down the window of their cab and breathed in the scent of the tide.

Yuriko turned slowly to look out the window. Squinting, she murmured, 'It's so pretty, isn't it?'

'Whenever I look at the sea, I remember that big fish,' said Izumi, feeling the salt breeze on his face.

'Big fish?' Yuriko shifted her gaze from the water to Izumi.

'The first time I went fishing. When I was in elementary school.'

'Oh, yes! And you caught a great big fish.'

'That's right. I was so shocked. I put some bait on the hook and a fish grabbed it as soon as I threw it in the water. I had to reel it in frantically.'

He moved his right hand, as though turning a reel, and Yuriko spread out her hands and said, 'It was huge. About thirty centimetres.'

'I went fishing a few times after, but never beat that record.'

'If nothing else, you've always had beginner's luck. The first time you got a raffle ticket, you won a bicycle, and you came first in your very first race at the school. But you know, Izumi, you're wrong.'

'About what?'

'You didn't catch that fish in the sea. We were at a lake,' she said, looking straight into his eyes. She was in unusually good shape today, speaking confidently. The two of them must have sounded like a typical mother and son. If the cab driver hadn't known their destination, he probably wouldn't have guessed that Yuriko had dementia.

'No, Mum, it was the sea. I remember clearly.'

'I can even tell you the name of that lake. And of the inn where we stayed. The fish you caught was a rainbow trout, and the inn grilled it with salt. Don't you remember? You kept saying it was delicious.'

Now that she mentioned it, maybe it had been a lake after all, he thought. He remembered being on the water in a rowboat and catching that fish. He could recall with a strange clarity the rocking of the boat and the saltiness of the grilled trout, but nothing else. His mother's memory was probably right.

Ever since her diagnosis, Izumi had made a point of talking to his mother about the past. He shared one anecdote after another, going back to the time he was old enough to remember. He felt it might somehow help hold down her memories as her symptoms progressed.

A picture book he'd begged her to read every night, about a boy and a bunch of monsters. Carrots stewed with butter and sugar. A blue toy car missing one of its side mirrors. The mini tomato plant he'd grown in the garden, only to have it become infested with aphids and wither away. An artistic classmate who was always drawing manga. The stuffed panda he couldn't bring himself to throw away until he graduated from elementary school. Just as he'd mistaken the lake for the sea, his mother's memories were usually more accurate, while his own often needed revising. It wasn't carrots but squash that she'd stewed with sugar. The toy car had been red, not blue.

His mother was in the process of forgetting, yet the vividness of the things she did remember constantly surprised him. Each time she corrected him, he realised how vague his own memories were; how often he'd rewritten them to suit himself.

Glancing down at her hands, he noticed she was clutching a flower-patterned pouch.

A birthday present he'd given her one year on New Year's Day. Probably when he was in the first year of junior high. She'd been thrilled and had kept it in her purse, taking it with her everywhere. After two decades, the colours had faded, but it was still well-kept, without any stains or grime.

'You still have that, Mum,' he said.

'Yes. It's my treasure.' Yuriko stroked the pouch with her hand.

She had lost it one day after Izumi entered senior high at fifteen. Her face pale, she'd searched all over the house. 'Where could I have dropped it,' she kept saying. For the next five days, she visited the local police *kōban* daily and scoured the streets between the house and the train station, but it didn't turn up.

'I'm so sorry, Izumi,' she said. 'You chose it specially for me.'

Izumi didn't mind and reassured her that it was okay, that it hadn't been expensive. But she became so despondent, she wouldn't get out of bed. Just as Izumi was wondering what to do, the police called to say the pouch had been found near the bus stop and was being kept for them.

They hurried over to the police box. His mother took the flower-patterned pouch from the officer and gripped it tightly in her slender white fingers. 'I promise I'll never lose it again,' she said.

In the cab, Izumi suddenly wondered what she kept in it. Come to think of it, he'd never seen the inside. He was seized by an urge to take a peek.

The cab turned off the coastal road into the lane, and the tiled roof of the old house came into view through the windscreen. That building would be his mother's home from now on. Beside him, Yuriko stared ahead, motionless. She must have been nervous. Her fingers trembled as she gripped her pouch, and Izumi was overcome with the feeling he was abandoning her. He found himself making excuses like 'I'll come see you on weekends,' even though she hadn't said anything.

'It's okay,' she said. 'You're busy at work, and your baby's coming soon.' She smiled gently as though she knew what he was feeling.

The director and her daughter were standing outside the door of Nagisa Home, waiting.

They unloaded Yuriko's luggage from the trunk, opened the door and took her things inside. Mizuki's daughter guided them around the facility, walking slowly along the wood floor. 'This is the bathroom, and here's the toilet. The staffroom is over there. We all eat meals together at the dining table.' Yuriko followed, repeating after her while pointing at each spot. 'This is the bathroom. Here's the toilet . . .' Walking behind, Izumi watched her small frame move from one side of the corridor to the other.

They walked up the creaky wooden stairs to the second floor, where Mizuki's daughter introduced Yuriko to the resident of each room. 'Nice to meet you, I'm Yuriko Kasai.' Some residents weren't able to respond, but Yuriko greeted each one politely and gave them a package of cookies she'd brought.

'This is your room, Mrs Kasai.' Mizuki's daughter opened the door of the room on the corner of the second floor. When they pulled back the curtains, the dark blue of the sea was visible beyond a daikon patch.

Mizuki joined them. 'You're so lucky, Mrs Kasai,' she said with a smile. 'This is the only room with a view of the sea.' Yuriko chewed over the words 'the only room', then gave a relieved smile.

The room was about the size of six tatami mats, and it didn't take long to unpack Yuriko's belongings and put them away. A few changes of clothes packed into a Boston bag and a single-flower vase. Make-up and a toothbrush. A pocket radio, a hair dryer and a few other electrical appliances. When they finished, Izumi sat down beside Yuriko on the bed and stared silently at the summer sea in the distance. Perhaps the number of a person's possessions is proportionate to the number of memories, he thought. As we approach death, we need less and less.

After Mizuki explained the daily routines at Nagisa Home, Izumi prepared to leave. The westering sun shone on the sea. Yuriko and Mizuki stood side by side at the entrance, waiting for Izumi's cab to arrive.

As soon as it came in sight, Yuriko said in a ringing tone, 'Please take good care of me,' and bowed deeply to Mizuki and Izumi, exposing the nape of her neck beneath her grey hair.

'We're looking forward to having you with us, Mrs Kasai,' Mizuki said, her face beaming as she took Yuriko by the arm. 'Izumi, please come and visit anytime.'

'Yes. I will,' Izumi answered in a small voice, his eyes fixed on the yellow body of the approaching cab. He couldn't look at his mother.

He dove into the taxi and asked the driver to head for the station. As the door closed, he thought he saw Yuriko's lips moving. She seemed to be trying to tell him something, but the taxi pulled away before he could figure out what it was. Watching her receding figure in the rearview mirror, he thought he heard her whisper in his ear, 'Bring me a flower, will you?'

Burned pots piled in the cupboard under the stove, plates stacked randomly in the dish cupboard, snacks stuffed into a paper shopping bag. Izumi returned to Yuriko's little house, now devoid of its owner, and cleared up her things. As he threw away Tupperware filled with stewed sun-dried daikon and cubes of braised pork from the freezer, he wondered how many times he'd eaten his mother's cooking. For a while, he stared at the food defrosting in the rubbish, somehow reluctant to part with any of it.

Once he finished cleaning out the kitchen, he went into the bathroom and gathered up his mother's massive stock of shampoo, detergent and soap. He thought of taking these home, but they didn't seem to belong in an apartment about to welcome a newborn baby, and he decided to throw them out instead. The overgrown garden, the messy shoe cabinet, closets overflowing with stuff. Although reluctant to intrude uninvited into Yuriko's private life, he didn't feel right leaving the job to a stranger. He couldn't find any albums or pictures from his childhood, then remembered he'd thrown them all away that day. He'd taken every photo in the house and chucked them into the bin as though giving up.

Before Izumi knew it, dusk had fallen. As lights flickered on in the windows of the nearby apartment blocks, he turned his attention to the bookcase, which he'd left untouched. Behind a row of paperback detective novels by such authors as Agatha Christie, Ellery Queen and Arthur Conan Doyle, which he knew his mother enjoyed, were old guidebooks to places like New York, London, India and Turkey. Even though she'd never travelled overseas. On that shelf, he'd stumbled across a longing he hadn't known his mother held.

He threw away almost everything that belonged to him – fashion and music magazines, CDs of alternative rock bands, DVDs of independent films. But he couldn't bring himself to discard any of his mother's books. Although he couldn't imagine she would ever read a mystery or guidebook again, he feared that throwing them out would make her recede even further from him.

A chaotic pile of household appliance manuals and warranties, New Year's cards and letters lay on top of the bookcase. As he began taking them down one by one to sort through them, a bundle of paper scraps fell to the floor.

Covered in words penned in his mother's familiar slender script.

Yuriko Kasai.
Born January 1st.
    My son's name is Izumi. He likes sweet rolled omelette and hayashi rice. He works at a record company. Mrs Nikaido the helper will come at 10:00. Don't buy bread. No more lessons with Miku. Izumi's wife is Kaori. Don't forget to buy a flower. The toilet is by the bedroom. I ate supper. Don't cause Izumi any trouble. I will take care of myself. Buy baby clothes as a gift. Buy light bulbs, AA batteries and toothpaste.

How did I end up like this?
Izumi, I'm so sorry.

Memory fragments that Yuriko had tried to tie down spilled from the memos. He heard her voice at Nagisa Home, reciting over and over, 'This is the bathroom. Here's the toilet.' He saw her figure in the cab's rearview mirror receding into the distance as she stood staring after him, looking forlorn.

Large drops of water splashed onto the scraps of paper on the floor. Sobs escaped him as he was seized by some perplexing emotion, whether grief or regret or something else, he couldn't tell. Ignoring the tears that ran down his cheeks, he gathered up the fallen memos, one by one, with trembling hands.

The last thing he opened was a box that had been shoved into the back at the bottom of the closet.

It contained an unfamiliar single-pearl pendant and two diaries.

Their black covers bore only the year: 1994 and 1995.

Of plain design, like those used by middle-aged men. He guessed his mother had chosen them for their plainness. He flipped through the pages and noticed that while the diary for 1994 had an entry almost every day, the one for 1995 had only a few entries. The rest of the days were blank.

The smell of miso soup engulfed him once again, and he clamped his hands over his nose and mouth.

Yuriko had vanished.

On a snowy day in April, just before Izumi entered the second year of junior high. She had made breakfast like every other morning, then said she was going out.

That day, his mother had abandoned him.

As he flipped through the pages, memories came flooding back. The things he had tried to forget. The year that he and Yuriko had erased.

3 April

'Where do you want these, Mrs Asaba?'

I froze when he called me that. Without waiting for an answer, the moving man, a huge fellow, kicked off his trainers, their heels squashed from being stepped on, and crossed the doorsill into the apartment. He grasped two cardboard boxes, stacked one on top of the other, in bear-like gloved hands. The sleeves of his white T-shirt were rolled up to his shoulders, baring bulging muscles.

'Over there,' I stammered, pointing to the bedroom. He stacked the boxes like a set of building blocks. It only took him three trips from the truck to the apartment to carry everything in.

When he was done, he asked me to sign the form. I grasped the ballpoint pen and wrote the unaccustomed surname 'Asaba'.

Asaba was in the living room trying to hook up the TV. Once the moving man had left, Asaba muttered that he was no good at this kind of thing. Even though you're a science major, I teased, and he smiled bashfully. I like his smile. His whole face crinkles up in a boyish grin.

It didn't take long to finish vacuuming. Other than the little kitchen, there are just two rooms: a small bedroom facing the train tracks and a living-dining room. Having lived in a house for so long, I was surprised by how easy this place is to clean.

'It's working!' Asaba shouted.

The news came on the TV screen, which Asaba had placed in a corner of the bedroom. The local newscaster, an unfamiliar face, reported on a hurricane in the south-eastern United States. A grey tornado funnel ripped the tin roof off a farmhouse and hurled it into the sky.

Asaba and I went to the supermarket in front of the station.

'What shall we have for supper? Ginger pork, *nikujaga*, mackerel simmered in miso? Or how about curry on rice?'

This would be my first time to cook for Asaba. We discussed what to eat while randomly grabbing things like vegetables, meat and fish and putting them into the shopping basket. Asaba walked ahead. In his basket was a big bottle of soy sauce and a bag of rice, as well as miso, salt and butter.

It hit me then – I'll be cooking for him every day from now on. We'll sleep together and wake together. It seemed unreal, like a dream. Only the weight of the food-laden basket told me it was true.

We walked side by side along the tracks, both of us clutching plastic shopping bags, one in each hand. It was already quite dark, and our breath turned white in the air. It still gets chilly at night.

'Yuriko, do you mind if I stop in there?' He paused and motioned with his hand, the heavy bag dangling from it.

Up ahead I saw a small bookshop, all alone under the elevated railway tracks. An incandescent glow seeped from beneath the faded red plastic awning over the shop front.

Gently, we slid back the glass door and stepped inside. Although small, it was neat and tidy, and free of the musty smell of most old bookshops. There weren't many bookshelves, but everything on them, from novels to magazines, seemed to have been carefully chosen by the shop owner as something customers should read.

An elderly woman sat alone behind the till at the end of the curated shelves. I heard the faint sound of a radio. Was she the owner? Back rounded, she sat so still she seemed like an ornament. She gave no sign that she noticed customers had entered. But because she was there the bookshop existed. That was how she made me feel.

Asaba walked slowly around the shelves twice, then picked out three pocketbooks. All historical novels. He showed them to me and said, as if poking fun at himself, 'An old man's choice?'

I glimpsed his white teeth between his thin lips. Everything about him is white. His face is white and smooth. His hands too are so pale I can see his veins stretching right down to his fingertips.

Though he has a slight stoop, he still stands a head taller than me and his limbs are long. He always wears a grey suit, and on holidays, a white shirt with a jacket.

He told me it's because he doesn't have much fashion sense. He doesn't want to fuss about what he wears, so he always chooses the same type of clothes, like an extension of a school uniform.

I suppose he does seem like an 'old man' in some ways. Maybe that's why I feel comfortable with him.

He told me to get something for myself too, but I couldn't see any books I particularly wanted to read. Instead, I picked up a diary from a stack beside the cash register.

A black one with just the year stamped on the fake leather cover.

I decided to buy it. No one will notice such an 'old man's choice'. This life of ours, which has finally begun. No one must notice.

4 April

Asaba went to work.

He said he was going to stay on after the entrance ceremony to talk with the other professors about the curriculum for the new school year.

I opened my Boston bag and unpacked my underwear, blouses, dresses, a light coat and other clothes and stowed them in a set of plastic drawers in the closet. It didn't take long. I didn't bring any books, music scores, accessories or make-up with me. I left it all behind in that house – my piano, my students, everything precious.

I removed Asaba's clothes one by one from the stack of cardboard boxes. They smelled somehow sweet. His smell. It made me want to hug them close. He hadn't even been gone an hour and already I wanted to see him. If he knew, would he think I was weird?

The box at the bottom of the stack was full of articles and technical books related to ships. I placed them in the bookshelf against the wall, arranging them according to their height. Among them I found a CD. By the pianist Vladimir Horowitz playing Schumann. An album I recommended to Asaba around the time we first met. I wondered when he bought it. It made me happy to find it.

I love the way Horowitz makes the piano sing when he plays. He changes the tempo at will rather than being faithful to the score, and his performances combine both power and sensitivity, lingering forever in the mind. As someone who can only play with disciplined precision, I've always admired him.

This is the first time I've kept a diary since the last summer of senior high school.

And I didn't stick with it for long. Even though it was a diary, I was so worried someone might read it, I soon tired of it.

I never thought of keeping a diary after that. I was too busy just living. I feel like I must have forgotten a lot of important things, but if I can't remember them, then they probably weren't such a big deal after all.

Now, however, I feel impelled to write.

I want to take everything I see and feel and tie it down somewhere. Asaba's almond-shaped eyes, his soft voice, his habit of rubbing his ear with his slender fingers. I'll write it all down here.

5 April
When I stepped onto the tiny veranda to hang the laundry, it started to rain.

There's nowhere else to hang things, so I brought them inside and gazed at the socks dangling from the clothespins.

My socks hung at intervals between Asaba's, and I realised with surprise how much bigger his feet are than mine.

From our window on the fifth floor, I can see the trains passing along the elevated tracks. The two-tone cream and vermilion cars are somehow familiar and dear. Two rows of trains are standing by in the rail yard beyond the station. Wet with rain, they wait faithfully for their turn to work.

It was raining the day I first met Asaba too.

A Saturday evening. I had finished Yuko's lesson and was watching the rain hit the window. I needed to go shopping for dinner, but it was raining so hard, I didn't want to go out.

That's when he came, his grey suit drenched by the rain. 'I want to learn piano,' he said shyly. 'I want to play something at my friend's wedding.'

He lived in the housing estate up the hill from my house and taught at a university at the next station. He told me that every time he passed my house and saw the sign, he stopped to listen to the piano.

'What piece do you want to learn?' I asked, and he said he liked Schumann. Many people listen to Chopin and Mozart, but Schumann is unusual. I'm one of those oddities too.

Happy to have found a like-minded person, I asked, 'Did you know that Schumann wrote music for the woman he loved?'

'The pianist Clara, right?' Asaba responded immediately. 'He sent her love letters and kept composing pieces for her.'

'It's touching, isn't it? And they even got married in the end. What's your favourite piece?'

'"Träumerei."'

Pleased again by this answer, I laughed and nodded in agreement. Perhaps my voice rose a little. 'Movement No. 7 of *Kinderszenen*'. It's my favourite too. Do you know the story behind it?'

'Didn't he write it for his children?'

'You would think so, wouldn't you?' I said. He gazed at me quizzically, as if begging me to continue. 'Schumann wrote it before he married Clara. Clara's father opposed their marriage, so Schumann secretly sent her love letters. One day, Clara wrote back, "Sometimes you seem like a child." *Kinderszenen* was inspired by those words.'

Asaba laughed like a little boy who has discovered a treasure. 'So, he really did compose all his pieces for Clara,' he murmured, tapping his fingers as though playing the piano. A silver band, still new, gleamed on the ring finger of his left hand.

From then on, Asaba came to my place every Saturday evening to practice 'Träumerei'. He played this one piece over and over so that he could perform it at his friend's wedding three months later. His fingers were long and dexterous, and he advanced quickly. He bought an electric piano so he could practise at home as well. I was impressed by his diligence. But what made me happiest of all was that he liked piano.

I've always lived in a house with a piano. Even when I was a child, we had a grand piano in the living room.

There is no piano in this small apartment. But I don't miss it.

6 April

I asked Asaba to tell me his teaching schedule.

Almost every day, he'll leave the house at nine and finish around five.

On Thursdays, he teaches from eleven. On Wednesdays, until three.

'Which means we can eat together every morning and evening, you see?' He said what I was thinking before I could.

In the evening, I washed all the newly bought dishes one by one and placed them in the glass-doored dish cabinet beside the kitchen.

It makes my heart flutter to see the dishes and cups, two of each kind, arranged side by side.

Tonight, I'll make beef stew for dinner.

11 April

After Asaba left for the university, I decided to stroll around the neighbourhood. Pink cherry petals carpeted the surface of a small river near our apartment.

The mountains ranging off into the distance were lush green. In the opposite direction, I glimpsed the sea. The city tilts gently down the mountain towards it.

Turning my eyes to the coast, I saw a row of large sake breweries. I'd seen the logo, a flying crane, on TV before. This must be where the company started.

From the nearest station, I climbed the gentle slope along the river, and an old public hall came into view. The faded brown building was topped by an observation deck that looked like a round hat.

It was lunchtime, so I ate lunch at an old diner in the basement of the public hall. Steam rose from the *omurice*, bright yellow on a velvety sauce. The elderly chef in the kitchen told me that this had been the diner's signature dish for more than sixty years. The omelette melted in my mouth, the mellow flavour of the eggs fusing with the sweet demi-glace sauce and the tangy ketchup-flavoured rice. I shovelled one spoonful after another into my mouth, polishing it off in no time, then downed my glass of water in a single gulp. It was delicious.

Next time, I'll invite Asaba to come with me, I thought. I want to bring him here. Suddenly, I couldn't stay still anymore, and before I knew it, I was on the train heading to his university. It's five stations away from our apartment, but the distance between each is so short that I reached the fifth station in just ten minutes.

A five-minute walk from there towards the sea. The campus came into view at the end of an enormous elevated expressway. Students were pouring from the university gates. They were almost all male, probably because the campus is dedicated to marine engineering. I kept my eyes down as I passed through the gate, ashamed of the sudden impulse, so unbecoming of my years, that had driven me there.

I slipped by the security guard when he wasn't looking and stepped quietly onto the campus grounds.

A silver observatory gleamed atop a white building. All the buildings on the campus were about three storeys high with benches in front of them. No students sat on the benches.

Walking past the buildings, I came to a sports field. Beige-coloured dirt stretched off into the distance. Students ran across it, practising soccer, rugby or track and field, but it seemed far too big for the number of people using it.

A boat, pristine white, lay docked at the small port beyond this beige expanse.

'The university I'll be teaching at has a big boat.'

I recalled how happy Asaba had looked when he told me this.

April 12

Yesterday's story continued.

I sat down on a bench by the sports field and gazed for a while at the white boat.

I wondered if Asaba would board it one day and sail off to sea. To Asia, or Europe, or even Africa. This thought made me feel lonely. Loneliness just won't let me go.

Before I knew it, the sun had begun to set.

'Yuriko, you came.' I heard a soft, low voice behind me. Turning, I saw Asaba looking down at me.

'I just finished my lecture and stepped outside. I was surprised to see someone who looked like you sitting there.'

Smiling, he came and sat beside me. Now that we're living in a strange place, we both seem to have become a little bolder.

'Why did you decide to study ships?' Sitting beside Asaba and gazing at the white boat, I remembered something I had always wanted to ask him.

He paused for a moment thinking, then said, 'I really wanted to be an architect. But I failed the exam and went into engineering instead. From there, I found my way to ships. I've always liked means of transport, especially boats. Cars are mass-produced, but ships are built one by one, just like houses.'

When speaking about his work, Asaba always talks fast. As if it makes him so happy, he's in a rush to share. I wonder if he knows that.

'The airplane was invented in 1903 and the car in 1769. But boats have been around for five thousand years. In ancient Egypt, they carried stones down the Nile River. The stones for the walls of Edo and Osaka castles were also carried by boat.'

I like boats, too. I never get tired of watching them from the shore. When I told him this, he started talking even faster.

'In my field, the study of fluid dynamics, a boat's propeller is very important. You can improve fuel efficiency just by slight alterations to the shape of the propeller. But the study of that field is endless. For example, there are still unresolved questions about the Navier-Stokes equations, which concern basic principles of fluid dynamics.'

After this rush of words, he fell silent for a while. I said nothing, just watching him. Maybe that was a little unkind.

His mouth twisted in a smile, and he murmured, 'I guess this topic isn't very interesting, is it?'

I cradled his hand in mine and told him that I enjoyed learning new things from him.

15 April

Once, after one of his piano lessons, Asaba and I talked about our parents.

I told him I'd been estranged from mine since I became a single mother.

Asaba's father was a scholar like him. He left when Asaba was five, choosing to work abroad rather than stay with his family.

'When my father left for Europe, we went to the port to see him off. My mother stood beside me, crying and waving. I knew then he was abandoning us.'

Still sitting on the bench in front of the piano, he went on. 'The whistle blew, and as the ship pulled away from the pier, streamers of different colours were thrown from the deck. It was so beautiful. I watched the ship through the dancing rainbow of streamers as it sailed off into the turquoise sea. The sadness of being abandoned by my father converged with the beauty of that scene and morphed into a love for ships. Weird, right?'

From my seat at the dining table, I slowly shook my head.

I knew exactly how he felt.

There are times when sorrow fuses with the beauty of a scene, transforming that sadness into love.

Talking with Asaba is always like discovering a single truth together.

I often feel we're like two explorers, one who traversed the southern hemisphere and the other who traversed the northern hemisphere. Once we met, we knew the whole world.

19 April

I bought some guidebooks at the bookshop under the railway tracks.

The old lady who owns the shop must think I'm a strange woman for buying so many. London, New York, India, Turkey.

I imagine myself travelling the world with Asaba.

What would happen if I went to Istanbul with him?

We would see the Blue Mosque and shop at the bazaar. After eating a mackerel sandwich, we'd enjoy smoking a water pipe. Would we be tricked into buying a Turkish carpet by a friendly guide or have our wallets stolen by a pickpocket and end up panicked and penniless?

Even so, as long as I was with him, I'm sure I'd still be happy.

I've finally met someone special.

Asaba. There's a lock of hair at the back of his head on the left that always stands up.

Is it a natural wave? From the time he gets up in the morning until he goes to bed at night, just that one spot is always rebelling. I bet Asaba doesn't know about that unruly lock. He hasn't noticed yet.

But if I tell him, it will no longer be just mine. So, I won't.

27 April

Around five o'clock in the evening, the refrain from Dvořák's 'Goin' Home' comes from a loudspeaker somewhere, the signal for children playing with their friends to go home.

I used to hear that melody every evening from my second-floor room in the big house we lived in. It seemed to say, Farewell, we'll meet again, I'm back.

When it finished, I could always smell the miso soup my mother was cooking.

Ah, it's almost supper time. Asaba will be coming home soon.

I better start preparing.

Tonight, I'll make ginger pork and miso soup with daikon.

Asaba is a very picky eater.

I found that out the first time we ate together. He hates green vegetables like lettuce and spinach, and he doesn't like squid, octopus or shellfish. He can't eat liver or giblets either.

After his father went abroad, his mother was too busy working to make him meals very often.

'She just gave me some money, and I bought whatever I liked,' Asaba said awkwardly when I looked at the green vegetables he'd pushed to one side of his plate.

He's left-handed. Just like my boy.

At night, the trains that have finished work roll back into the rail yard in droves.

Out the window, I can see their lights, eight rows of them lined up in their sheds.

It's like a train hotel.

2 May

That night, I lied and said I was going out to meet a friend from high school. Asaba had invited me out for dinner to thank me because his performance of 'Träumerei' at his friend's wedding had been a great success.

We met up in a busy part of town some distance away and headed towards the restaurant where we planned to eat. But it was closed for renovations.

Asaba apologised for not calling to reserve ahead of time, then asked me to wait while he hurried off to look for another restaurant. I stared after his ungainly figure as he disappeared into the bustling night-time shopping district.

A few minutes later, he returned out of breath with a frown on his face. 'There are several restaurants, but I was so flustered I couldn't decide which one would be good.'

I burst out laughing. I found him funny, but also endearing. He wiped the sweat from his brow with a puzzled expression on his face.

I suggested a restaurant in the station building that served *yōshoku* cuisine, and we decided to have Hamburg steaks. We laughed as we raised our white napkins to protect ourselves from the juices that spit from the sizzling iron platters.

Asaba asked me many questions. What kind of child was I? Why did I start learning piano? What romantic relationships had I experienced? 'You fascinate me, Mrs Kasai,' he said with a boyish smile.

I couldn't answer his questions properly.

I just kept saying that I didn't remember. It wasn't that I didn't want to answer. In fact, I was sure with Asaba, I'd feel quite comfortable talking about it. But when I tried to recall things, the details were unclear, as though covered in mist, and I couldn't put them into words.

'I can't seem to remember anything about myself. Even though I can remember every little detail about my son.' I sipped the espresso which had been served after the dessert. It was a bitter-tasting dark roast. 'I guess I was so focused on just surviving with my boy that I didn't give much thought to myself.'

Asaba gazed into my face intently the whole time. Taking a deep breath, he said, 'From now on then, why don't you try living for yourself? At least when you're with me.'

A lively piano piece came over the speakers. Waltz in C# minor by Chopin. An undanceable waltz.

Asaba focused so intently on playing the right notes that he always tensed up. Every time, I encouraged him to enjoy the music more. After all, I reminded him, the Japanese characters for the word 'music' mean 'to enjoy sound'.

'You're right,' he always said with a crooked smile, then glared at the music again as soon as he began pressing the keys. Watching him, I felt that music, in every way, reflects the person who plays it.

Asaba is someone who can't step outside the box.

Me too.

We can't let ourselves ad lib.

We can only place one note carefully on top of the other.

As I listened to the piece in the restaurant, I realised it was played by Horowitz. The sound was light yet so powerful, it gave me the push I needed.

I would try living for myself.

The fog seemed instantly to lift.

Ever since I'd resolved to live for my child, my time, my money and my heart had no longer belonged to me. I thought I was fine with that. But maybe when I was with

Asaba, it would be all right to live for myself. Just when I was with him.

As we left the restaurant, he said, 'Let's make lots of memories together.'

By the time I realised it, we were in a hotel room. At my invitation.

3 May

I'm not good at accepting kindness. I can't help thinking people are being kind because they feel sorry for me as a single mother, and that's hard for me to accept.

But Asaba isn't kind like that.

He's just there, quietly beside me.

'I got a job in Kobe.'

Asaba announced this abruptly. In bed, while hugging me from behind. Half a year had passed since we'd begun seeing each other.

Why? When? What should I do? All these questions rose in my mind, but all I said was, 'Uh-huh.'

He was being hired as a professor by a new university. His wife and child would stay behind while he rented an apartment in Kobe. He murmured these things in my ear as though talking to himself.

Asaba doesn't know how to be tactful, eloquent or adroit in his dealings with others. He's earnest pure-hearted and boyish.

At the same time, he lacks compassion for others, no matter who they are. There's something absent-minded about everything he says, which makes it hard to grasp what he really feels. But for me, this innocent heartlessness seems just right.

To the very end, Asaba never asked me to come with him.

He never decides anything. It is always me who decides. What to eat, where to go, when to meet. But he always says, 'That's a good idea,' to whatever I suggest. He accepts me as I am. Even if I told him we should break up, he'd probably look a little sad but just say, 'I guess it can't be helped.'

And here I am. With Asaba.

I thought I'd live the rest of my life with my boy. I believed that solitary island was all I needed. But then I discovered the world.

A white ship wandered into my secluded little harbour. From the deck, Asaba called me, and I jumped aboard. I didn't know where the ship was going.

But that didn't matter.

9 June
I've been here alone ever since Asaba went home.

I spend my time counting the planes crossing the blue sky or the trains passing along the tracks. Though I stay this way, the world carries on without me.

Inside, anxiety at being left behind melds with a strange relief, immobilising me.

As I sorted through the scattered post, my eyes fell on a stamp with a picture of a white-eye and a crested king-fisher. Postcard stamps are 50 yen. Letters are 80. Come to think of it, postage fees went up at the beginning of the year. I realise that I haven't sent postcards or letters for the past six months.

I think about writing a letter and pick up a pen.

But to whom? My pen halts.

Because I chose Asaba.

That's what I tell myself.

13 June

Asaba returned in the evening.

He placed his leather travel bag in the entranceway and embraced me from behind while I stood in the kitchen cutting the tofu for the miso soup.

He kissed my neck again and again, caressing my waist with both hands. Behind me, I heard the sound of his belt being unbuckled. 'Wait,' I said, but he began unbuttoning my blouse as if he hadn't heard. His ragged breathing touched my ear, and the longing I had forgotten during these last few days came rushing back. My knees felt weak, and my legs shook. Those fingers, that voice, the scent of his skin, were all so dear.

While lying naked on the futon, Asaba noticed the goldfish bowl.

I told him I bought the bowl and the fish at the tropical fish shop one station over. A small fantail goldfish and a slightly larger one of the same species. I bought them as a pair, so they wouldn't be lonely. I named the two bright-red fish Momiji and Kaede.

10 July

Asaba has been staying up all night the last few days. He seems to have a lot of research to do and papers to write and stays shut up in his lab until morning.

When I sleep by myself, I dream a lot. Scary dreams, sad dreams, happy dreams. In almost all of them, I'm alone. But Asaba joined me in last night's dream, and that made me happy. Yet I can't remember where we were or what we did together.

That seems like a waste. From now on, I'll write my dreams down.

I've heard that everyone dreams daily. We just don't remember. All those dreams we've forgotten. What was in them, I wonder.

3 August

I went into town to get ready for Asaba's birthday.

'Yuri-chan?' someone said while I was choosing cake in the basement food floor of the department store. It was Y, a classmate from music college. A high-bridged nose and sculpted cheekbones, like someone half white, a childlike voice, slender arms and legs. Despite the wrinkles visible around her eyes and neck, her doll-like appearance was surprisingly unchanged from when we were students together. The only indication that two decades had passed since then were her daughters, who resembled her closely. They walked beside her, one on her right and the other on her left.

'So, it is you, Yuri-chan! You haven't changed a bit!' As I stood there, frozen, she asked, 'What are you doing in Kobe?'

The name of the geographical location jogged my memory.

Y had married as soon as she graduated from college and moved to Kobe when her husband was transferred there.

The class mood-maker, cheerful and cute with a boisterous laugh. She got smashed at her farewell party and went up to each classmate with tears in her eyes, urging them to come see her in Kobe and go out for Kobe beef.

'My husband's working in Kobe now too . . .' Like a reflection in a mirror, I claimed to be in the same situation as her. 'So, we've moved here as a family.'

'Really! How long have you been here?'

'Uhm, since last year maybe.'

'Great. Do you have any kids?'

'A boy. He's already in junior high.'

Having said that much, I suddenly realised that I hadn't met any of my college classmates since I gave birth. And of course, I hadn't told any of them either.

'A boy? Which junior high?'

'Um, it's in Ishiyagawa.' Caught off balance, I blurted out the name of our station.

'Ishiyagawa? Is there a junior high there?'

At a loss for words, I looked around. Cakes topped with colourful fruits were lined up in the showcase in front of me. Despite my predicament, I was still thinking about which cake would please Asaba. I said nothing, and Y continued talking.

'Ah, it must be Mikage Junior High. How nice. With such a kind and gentle mother as you, I'm sure he must love you so much he can't stand to be apart.'

'No, not at all. He's reached the rebellious stage, and he's got more energy than he knows what to do with.'

'My daughters too. They aren't girls anymore but women – and quite precocious.'

Y flicked her eyes towards her daughters, who were about the same height as her. They had already wandered off and begun examining a kiosk selling chocolates a short distance away.

'But girls are always their mother's allies. I envy you.'

'You may think so, but one day they'll get married and leave home.'

'Boys are the same, you know. Once they get married, they don't come back.'

Before I realised it, we were engaged in typical mum talk. In the basement of the department store, packed with goods and bustling with customers. In front of the showcase displaying colourful cakes, Y and I continued the kind of conversation I'd heard other mothers have before.

After graduating from music college, I became a piano teacher. I never made it as a pianist, but I couldn't bring myself to give up piano. Later, I married an assistant professor I met through a mutual friend. He studies ship propellers. I don't really understand what he does. I don't even really know what I'm doing now either. We bought an old house for the three of us, but when the university in Kobe hired my husband as a professor, we all moved here. At first, I didn't know what to do, but now that I'm used to it, I find it's a nice city. It's quiet, and the sea and mountains are beautiful. My husband and I often say we wish we could have lived here when our boy was younger. I quit teaching piano after moving here. I just play as a hobby now. But my son is really into electric guitar. It makes a lot of noise. He doesn't get any better, and I wonder if I should learn it myself and teach him how.

I laughed and joked and talked about 'my life' with ease. Lies and truth blended together so that I couldn't tell what was real and what wasn't. As I talked, I began to believe I'd really lived that life. If I rewrite my memories, they're all mine.

After reminiscing for about thirty minutes, Y and I parted, exchanging contact information before we left.

'Let's meet again!' Y waved a slender arm vigorously as she led her two daughters away. She looked like a mother. I wonder what I looked like.

Extravagant side dishes bought in the deli section of the department's basement food floor, homemade dishes, strawberry shortcake as birthday cake. Asaba ate them all with relish.

'I've reached the last year of my thirties,' he murmured. I still can't believe he's six years younger than me.

10 August

I never really think much about Asaba being younger than me, but when I see his sleeping face, I sometimes remember that he is.

Tomorrow, he goes home for three days.

11 August

Asaba goes home once every two months.

He probably sees his wife and son, but he never talks about it.

His home is there, not here.

If so, then what's this apartment? A perch where a bird briefly rests its wings?

As I wait alone, I recall how I felt before I gave birth.

At that time, I stayed inside and saw no one, my belly gradually swelling in size. Cleaning, washing clothes, cooking. I did the chores and played piano.

Bearing my child on my own. Those days weren't as lonely as I expected. They were filled with a joy that was all mine: the joy of nurturing a life.

But there were times I felt so alone and anxious, I couldn't sleep. On nights like that, I would go for a walk.

Ambling along the dark streets, I talked to the child in my belly. When you're born, what should we eat? Where should we go? What music should we listen to? I wonder if you'll like piano.

I lay alone on the hospital bed, gripped by excruciating labour pains.

My mother and father didn't come. With this slim hope dashed, I sank into gloom. Intense pains surged and receded like waves. I was curled up on the bed, trembling with helplessness when the obstetrician, an elderly man, came and said, 'The baby's working hard in there too.'

Hang in there. Hang in there, I urged myself and the baby as I lay on the bed.

The waves grew bigger, and the pain became almost unbearable. As I began to fade from consciousness, the nurse rushed in and wheeled me into the labour room.

In the stark white light, I clenched my teeth.

Two. Three.

The voice of the elderly doctor reached my ears. 'Keep going! You're almost there!'

I gripped the bars on the side of the bed and pushed. Sweat poured from my skin.

Four. Five. Six. I bore down as hard as I could.

Something warm emerged, as if the core of my being was being pulled from my body.

Wails burst forth.

'It's born! You did it!'

The doctor passed me a bright red baby.

Trembling, I cradled it in my arms. Warm and soft.

Thank you.

Before I realised it, tears were flowing down my cheeks.

Thank you. We've met at last. From now on, it'll be just the two of us.

Why did I go and write about that? I'm going to take a break from writing my diary for a while.

29 September

A thief broke into the corner apartment on the first floor.

The police even came to our place on the fifth floor and asked me several questions. Had I seen any strangers go in or out of the building? Had I heard any noise yesterday afternoon?

I said no to both questions. If I had searched my memory, I might have noticed something, but I wanted to keep that interview as short as possible.

The officer looked at me with eyes that said, 'We suspect you too, you know.' If he'd seen me with Asaba, would he have realised we weren't married?

I left the house right after and went to a coffeeshop in front of the station.

It's an old shop, and the showcase outside displays wax replicas of things like spaghetti Napolitan, fried eggs, toast and cream soda. The old man who runs it never talks to the customers except to take orders. It's the kind of place I can linger over a cup of coffee all alone for as long as I like without feeling uncomfortable.

A voice suddenly interrupted my thoughts. 'Seems that scary things really do happen, doesn't it?'

From the table next to mine, a man wearing tortoise-shell glasses and eating spaghetti with meat sauce was looking at me. The sound of a comedian delivering a rapid-fire monologue came from the television, which was perched high up on the wall like a Shinto house shrine.

'Was your place okay?'

Who is this man, I wondered. I stared at his familiar-looking face. As though realising something, he removed his glasses, revealing eyes with thick flat lids. It was the man who lives next door. Half a year has passed since we moved in, but I'd never had a conversation with him. We'd only greeted each other politely in passing. In a small voice, I said our place was fine.

'What a dangerous world it's becoming. Honestly,' the man muttered, as if to the television. Does the fact he's in this coffeeshop in the afternoon mean he's not working, I wondered. But I'd never heard any noises from next door during the day. I nodded slightly, and the man continued.

'But really, it's so bizarre.'

'Bizarre? What is?'

'I heard it from the caretaker, but it seems almost nothing of any value was stolen.'

'Really? Then what?'

'Family photo albums, worn-out bags and some souvenirs, like a carved wooden bear and pennants from different tourist locations.' He finished speaking and began eating his pasta, slurping it up like you would buckwheat noodles. The comedian on the TV was repeating the same gag over and over.

The man guffawed, his mouth still stuffed with pasta which made his voice sound muffled. 'That's hilarious. Cracks me up.' As if in agreement, the sound of canned laughter echoed around the shop.

Suddenly, I recalled a book I read once, a long time ago.

About grey men who come to a town where a young girl lives. They steal time. Not realising what's happening, the grown-ups begin working relentlessly. The girl, however, realises what's going on and tries to take back the stolen time.

I ran over the list of stolen items in my head. Family photo albums, used bags, a carved wooden bear, pennants. All of these are memories. A chill ran up my spine, and I glanced around the shop. My neighbour was no longer there. I saw my face reflected in the cup of coffee in front of me. I looked frightened.

When Asaba comes back, I'll tell him about the memory thief. He probably won't take me seriously though.

2 October
It was a nice day, so I took a walk along the river. I smelled a sweet, milky fragrance and glanced up to see tiny orange flowers blossoming.

'Fragrant olive.' The name passed my lips. This scent used to waft from the garden next door every autumn. We always sat side by side under the eaves of our house and inhaled the fragrance.

8 October

I had a fight with Asaba.

The reason was so trivial it's not even worth writing down. In fact, I don't even remember what it was.

We argued for about five minutes, then Asaba fell silent, sitting stonily at the dining table. Not wanting to be in the same space, I went into the bedroom and closed the door.

I heard the sound of the front door and peeked into the living room. No one was there. Asaba had gone out without saying anything.

Fine. Let him. He'll come back at some point, I thought, but when he still hadn't come back or even contacted me after two hours, I went out to look for him.

I guessed he would go either to the area around the station or the university. I walked to the station and looked in all the shops. I walked up and down the streets, bustling with the evening crowd, searching. But I didn't see him.

Not knowing what else to do, I got on the train and headed for the university. The sun was beginning to set, and I walked around the empty campus and peered into his laboratory, but I still couldn't find him.

By this time, my body was quite chilled, so I went home. The room was dark, and there was no indication that he'd returned. Had he gone back to Tokyo, leaving me behind? I told myself he wouldn't do that.

Not knowing what to do, I hurried over to the supermarket in front of the station and bought things for supper. I'll make him his favourite, Hamburg steak with sweet stewed carrots, I thought. I'm sure he'll tell me it's delicious.

I left the supermarket, my hands weighed down with two full shopping bags. Seeing the pharmacy right in front of it, I remembered we were out of tissues and ducked inside the bright fluorescent-lit store.

I grabbed some boxes of tissues and toilet roll from a stack at the entrance, then proceeded further inside. I shoved bottles of shampoo, soap, laundry detergent and fabric softener under my arms.

How long will it take us to use these up? Three months? Half a year? Would I even be with Asaba that long? Would the day come when I would buy us more shampoo?

Although my arms were full, I stopped in at the flower shop. While I was trying to pick a flower and a vase, I realised that I hadn't bought flowers even once since I'd come here.

Returning to our apartment, I found Asaba lying on his side on the tatami mats watching TV. A comedy trio shouted, 'You never told me!' while striking exaggerated poses.

Asaba laughed.

He was still laughing at a gag that had been popular last year. I remembered the neighbour in the coffeeshop.

He'd been laughing with his mouth full of pasta, but he didn't seem to be enjoying himself at all. Maybe that's Asaba's future.

Eyes still on the TV screen, Asaba murmured, 'Yuriko, I'm sorry.' He's not very good at apologising.

'I'm sorry too. I'll make supper right away,' I answered quickly, then rolled up my sleeves and went into the kitchen.

30 November

Asaba had a holiday, so we walked over to the diner in the basement of the public hall and ate *omurice*. It's so close, we could go any time. With that attitude, it has taken us half a year to get there.

Maybe it's human nature not to bother with things you can eat anytime. Or maybe it's Asaba's nature.

These days, we rarely go out together. We don't have sex either.

6 December

I can't seem to control this complicated thing called maternal instinct. This feeling resembling love, or pity, or pain, paralyses me.

Asaba doesn't have this problem. I sense no paternal instinct in him.

24 December

I went to Sannomiya to buy ingredients for Christmas Eve dinner. When I finished shopping, I had tea with Y at the department store's enclosed rooftop café. Since our chance meeting in August, we've kept in touch occasionally. This was our third time to meet in person.

The last time, and the time before that, I talked about my imaginary life. The difficulties of getting along with the neighbours, my son's accomplishments at the school sports day, complaints about my husband, preparations for going home for New Year's.

Stories emerge effortlessly whenever I talk with Y, even though I don't prepare anything in advance. Stories of life with my husband and only son, a life infused with happiness even though we aren't particularly wealthy.

Sometimes I want to talk about the truth too.

'The other day, there was a break-in at our apartment building, you know.'

'Really? Were you okay?'

'Uh-huh. The burglar only broke into the first floor. Our place was fine.'

'That's fortunate,' Y said, looking relieved as she plucked the strawberry from the top of her shortcake. She's a passionate person and expresses her feelings with every part of her attractive face.

'But it actually turned out to be not so fortunate.'

'Why's that?'

'Because our neighbour, who used to just greet me with a quick bow, now stops to talk all the time.' I inserted my fork in my cake, careful to avoid disturbing the strawberry. I envied Y, who could eat the strawberry first.

'That sort of thing's a pain, isn't it? I know it's immature, but if someone looks like they might head for the lift, I press the button to close the doors.'

'I'm the same. If I pass someone in the passageway of our apartment block, I can't say hello.'

'I know just what you mean! I can't believe people who can do that as if it's normal.'

'But isn't that what adults should do?' I say with a laugh.

'You're right,' Y says, and bursts out laughing too, covering her mouth with her hand. When we're together, I feel like we're both college students again. As if this has always been the place we belong.

'But the break-in was really peculiar. The burglar only stole photo albums, worn-out bags and travel souvenirs.'

'No money or bank books?'

'Didn't even touch them.'

'That's scary somehow.'

Y always throws the ball back to me exactly where I want it. When I told Asaba this story, he sounded bored. 'He was probably just in a hurry,' he said.

'Exactly. It's as if he was stealing the person's memories. Wouldn't it be creepy to have something like that stolen?'

'Uh-huh. Yuri, what would upset you the most if someone took it? I mean things like money can be replaced in the end, right?'

'My diary.'

I answered reflexively. If my diary was stolen, what would become of me? What would the person who read it think?

'You're so right! That would be the worst!' Y's voice grew excited.

'Do you keep a diary?' I asked, getting nosey. She nodded and I followed with another question. 'What kinds of things do you write about?'

Her smile vanished. Realising I'd overstepped the bounds, I sipped my tea quietly. She'd only eaten the strawberry and had not yet touched her cake. The strains of a foreign boys' choir singing 'Jingle Bells' played in the background.

'Actually Yuri . . . I've fallen in love.'

'You mean?'

'Uh-huh. We're having an affair. He's married too, but we meet practically every day. Just like teenagers, huh? But we love each other. I'd go crazy without him. But I can't tell anyone. That's why I'm writing a diary.'

'Me too.' The words escaped my lips. Me too. I started an affair with a piano student six years younger than me, left my son behind when my lover was transferred here for his job, as if we were eloping, and I'm living here in hiding with him.

'Me too.' I paused, then said, 'If I had the chance, I'd like to fall in love. So, I can really understand how you feel.'

At this false expression of empathy, Y smiled, but just with her lips. I heard the breath hiss through her slightly opened mouth, as if she were laughing under her breath.

Her smile seemed disdainful, as if to say, 'Why don't you just tell the truth instead of carrying on like this?'

As I listened to the boys' choir, I thought we'd probably never see each other again.

25 December

My little Christmas party with Asaba is over. He fell asleep right after, perhaps drunk on the champagne, which he's not used to drinking.

Alone, I read through my diary. My life in this town. Asaba. My feelings.

I realise there is a lot I haven't written. Even in this diary, I can't write the truth.

Am I going to lie here too, just like I lied to Y?

I don't want to write anything in here but the truth.

Once I start lying in my diary, there will be no end.

1 January

I greeted my birthday with Asaba.

I asked him if he shouldn't be going home for New Year's, but he said he was struggling to meet the deadline for a paper. Even before the year end, he was going to the university every day to write. Looks like it will continue this way right up to the end of the school year.

He spent today sitting at his desk too, but in the evening, he suddenly disappeared and came back with a cake he'd bought.

'I thought about it for days, but in the end, I couldn't decide what to get you,' he said, scratching his head. He gave me a necklace with a single pearl pendant. I wondered when he could have bought it. When I imagined him at the jewellery shop, shy and embarrassed, I couldn't help but find him adorable.

No one forgets my birthday, but they always forget me.

So, I think it's nice to have a birthday like this sometimes.

5 January

I've been working on jigsaw puzzles in the apartment. Asaba's not here. Over the last three days, I've completed the Statue of Liberty in New York and the Taj Mahal in India. Now I'm tackling the Tower Bridge in London.

Will I ever see the real thing? When I spend such a long time staring at a building like this, I feel like I've already been there many times.

In the evening, I stopped in at the bookstore. The old lady was sitting at the counter listening to the radio as usual. I bought an Agatha Christie. *And Then There Were None.* How many times have I bought this one? I've read it at least three times, but I always forget who did it.

On the way home, I stopped by the flower shop and bought a single-flower vase and a red tulip. In the autumn, I wasn't able to choose anything in the end. Today, however, it seemed easy to find the right flower.

16 January

When I brought in the laundry tonight, the sky was yellow. A deep dandelion yellow. In the distance, I could see the cranes in the industrial zone silhouetted against the sky like shadowgraphs.

Asaba will be staying at the university again tonight, working on his paper.

For some reason I can't sleep. As I stare at the fishbowl, Kaede and Momiji swim round and round, as if they're being chased.

When Asaba comes home tomorrow, I'll suggest we go out to eat eel to perk him up. Because he's bound to be tired.

✳ ✳ ✳

I wake as the ground heaves violently beneath me. The grain of the wood-panelled ceiling seems warped. I try to get up, but the floor flounders like a boat in a gale, and I can't stand. The entire room creaks and groans, as if it's being squeezed within a giant hand. The fish bowl falls on the floor and shatters. Two goldfish, bright red, flop about on the dark-brown flooring. The bookcase falls with a dull thud, and books and magazines slide across the tatami mat floor like an avalanche. Dishes fly through the glass doors of the cabinet, shattering as they hit the floor. A crack spreads through the wall, and a sharp mouldy odour pricks my nostrils.

My brain can't grasp what's happening, and there's no time to feel any fear. Without a sound, I curl up on the futon with the quilt over my head. About thirty seconds later, the shaking subsides. I throw off the quilt and rush to open the window.

There's no sound. No human voices, no chirping of birds, no rustling of trees in the breeze. I strain to see the outside world in the dim predawn light. The railroad tracks below me undulate like waves. The trains lined up in the train yard lie on their sides, scattered across the tracks like plastic toys.

Asaba's not here. I look at the clock. Five fifty. He would have stayed at the university until dawn, writing his paper. I pick up the phone and dial the number for his lab, but the call doesn't go through. Is he all right? I press the buttons on the phone again and again, but just get a busy signal. An image of a tsunami swallowing the campus flashes through my mind, and sweat beads my palms. Bile rises in my throat, and I clamp my hands over my mouth.

I throw on a nylon coat and run outside. I race down the outer stairway, the concrete of which is cracked, and head for the station. Others who have also escaped from their houses wander aimlessly about, still in their pyjamas.

I pass through the ticket gate at the station and climb the stairs to the platform. A derailed train, curved like a snake, sits alongside the tracks. I turn and make my way back down the stairs, then begin running towards the university, following the tracks. It's just five stations down the line. Even if I walk, I should get there within an hour. The concrete roadway is humped like a camel's back. A fissure runs down the median line, and fragments of pavement with orange paint lie scattered. The telephone poles lining the streets have been toppled like dominos, and an intricate tangle of power lines covers the sky like a spider's web.

Black smoke rises from a house, the first floor of which has been crushed, and I hear a voice screaming for help from inside. An old woman wrapped in a blanket sits along the side of the road muttering wordlessly. A man clutches two crying children, one under each arm, and walks round and round a park begging for water. A cat with soot-covered paws meows hoarsely at his feet. The road is littered with shattered tiles from the roofs of collapsed houses. The footing is so bad, I can't run. I keep walking, the broken tiles crunching under my feet.

Gradually, sound returns. The gasping of my breath and the pounding of my heart echo in my ears. I can't tell if the town has begun to emit noise again or if my hearing has returned.

An enormous box-like thing appears in front of me, blocking my path. Drawing closer, I see it's a five-storey apartment building that has been snapped off at the ground floor and toppled onto the road. Clothes and bedding, washing machines and air conditioners that have been flung from the rooms lie strewn along the street. It's as if the building has ejected all the lives within it. The signboard from a construction company on the first floor is stuck upside down in a crack in the concrete. Turned on end, the writing on it looks like hieroglyphs from some exotic land.

A crowd has gathered in a narrow street beside the apartment building. It's too dark to see clearly, but I can tell that people are being dragged from inside. Perhaps they're already dead: they're draped from head to toe in red blankets.

I see myself squashed flat while curled up under my quilt during that violent shaking. My father stands gazing down at my body. 'I told you so,' he says. Beside him, my mother just stands there weeping and saying, 'Poor thing.'

Who will love me? My father? My mother? Asaba? Who will shed heartfelt tears at the sight of my dead body when I die?

A middle-aged woman in a negligee cuts across my line of view. She's walking down the ruptured street with a dog, a Shiba, on a leash. It takes me a while to grasp the significance of her actions. I stare at her figure as it vanishes into the smoke billowing up from the ruins before finally realising that she's 'walking her dog'. Her behaviour appears insane. Yet even at a time like this, people try to carry on with life as though nothing has changed. Maybe I'm no different from her as I try to get to Asaba. Our minds are telling our bodies to carry on with life as usual.

I keep walking, though I'm out of breath. At least an hour must have passed. Is Asaba all right? The tennis court along the river comes into view. I'll be with him soon. Once I get past this, his university will be just up ahead. I quicken my pace, even though the cracks in the road make me stumble.

The sun rises against the grey sky. Thick black smoke blocks its light. The horizon is stained red. The town, the people, the sky are on fire.

In front of me lies a huge expressway flyover – a great concrete road turned on its side like a beached whale. The downed section must be five hundred metres, or even a kilometre long. Thick concrete columns look like they've been twisted and torn from their foundations.

There's a row of ten or more trucks alongside the collapsed piece of carriageway. They slid off and crashed into the trees along the boulevard. Oranges spill from the back of the last truck and lie scattered across the road. Beyond the fallen carriageway I see a church. A black cross rising above broken stained-glass windows leans drunkenly as it watches the sky.

Time seems to stand still. Like some made-up world in a sci-fi novel where everything has stopped. And within that world, only I am walking.

Asaba's university appears. If I walk for just a few more minutes, I'll be at the gate. Soon we'll be reunited. But I can't get my legs to move any farther. Gasping for breath, I come to a halt. The sweet, tangy scent of crushed oranges wafts my way, reaching my nose.

Suddenly, I'm screaming in the midst of the debris. For a while, I don't know what I'm saying. I just keep repeating the same word over and over, as if spitting it out. At last, I recognise it. My son's name. I have to go home. I have to go home to Izumi. My throat feels raw, and I cough. Tepid tears course down my cheeks.

Izumi . . . Izumi . . . Izumi!

Beneath a sky cloaked in thick black smoke, in the middle of the concrete rubble, I keep shouting his name.

11

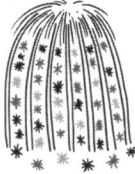

Izumi brought a plastic spoonful of golden pudding to Yuriko's lips. She'd always loved custard and was especially fond of cream puffs and pudding. Rather than classy versions made with whipped cream, she preferred simple custard pudding with a rich egg flavour.

Under the eaves of Nagisa Home, the cicadas' buzzing sounded strident and the resident dog lay with its tongue lolling. The rapid rise and fall of its side proclaimed the day to be brutally hot. Strong sunlight starkly separated the inside world from the outside, painting one black and the other white.

Like a baby bird waiting to be fed, Yuriko opened her mouth. Izumi slipped the spoon inside, and she downed the pudding in a single swallow.

'Good?' he asked.

She inclined her head with a smile. For some reason, the childish expression on her face reminded him that they were mother and son. 'It's so good, Izumi,' she kept saying.

As he wiped her lips with a cloth, he thought she'd probably done the same for him when he was a baby. They'd switched roles, that was all.

Yuriko choked. Beside him, Kaori held out a glass of iced barley tea. Her belly, which had swelled to the size of a basketball, bulged beneath her dress. The obstetrician had said the baby would be born at the end of the month. Kaori had come today because once she gave birth, she wouldn't be able to come for a while.

Yuriko drank the tea, then bowed her head and said, 'Thank you so much for coming all this way, Mrs Nikaido.'

'This is Kaori, Mum.'

'That's right. Miku. You've grown so much. Can you play "Träumerei" well now?'

'Mum, like I said. This is Kaori, my wife.'

'Really? How wonderful, Izumi. What a nice girl you found.' His mother reached over and grasped Kaori's hand. She was unusually talkative today. 'How kind of you to come and visit me together,' she continued. 'When Izumi gets hungry, Miku, he becomes quite grumpy. Did you know that?'

'I know just what you mean. What did you do when he was like that?' Kaori asked, matching her conversation to whatever Izumi's mother said.

Yuriko chattered on happily. 'Feed him. Anything will do. I used to give him a banana before dinner.'

'Is that right? I'll have to make sure we never run out of bananas then.'

The two laughed together. 'Thank you so much for coming,' Yuriko said, tears suddenly spilling from her eyes. According to the staff, she cried like this almost every day now.

At the table beside them, other residents were taking mangetout from a colander, destringing them and putting them in a metal bowl. They talked animatedly about their favourite singers or figure skaters, acting like a group of teenage girls who'd aged without growing up. Their hands worked deftly, flicking the vivid green mangetout into the bowl one after another. Izumi remembered Mizuki saying that people tend to retain memories of procedures. From the corner of his eyes, he watched the group of women while continuing to place dollops of pudding on Yuriko's tongue.

Over the last few weeks, Yuriko's symptoms had seemed to progress. The doctor who came to give Nagisa residents regular check-ups had told Izumi the disease might be advancing more rapidly because his mother was relatively young. 'She's still quite healthy physically, though, and I recommend you talk to her a lot,' he'd said.

Since then, Izumi had made a point of coming to see his mother every Sunday, but he noticed she spoke less and less after moving into the home. By simply responding 'Yes' or 'No' to suggestions about food or activity choices and times, she could get away with using a limited number of words. This lack of verbal interaction made Izumi feel lonely, as if his mother was going somewhere and leaving him behind, but he could also see that giving up words freed his mother from thinking. Ironically, he found it easier to talk with her once she could no longer carry on a proper conversation. In the past, conversations with her had felt suffocating; now it seemed simple to keep the ball rolling.

'Mum, it looks like our baby will be born this month. Who do you think it will look like? Me or Kaori?' Izumi had asked his drowsy mother this question the previous Sunday after lunch.

'Hmm. I wonder,' she'd murmured. She might have been answering him or just mumbling in her sleep.

'Do I look like my father? After all, you and I don't look at all alike.'

No one had ever told him he resembled his mother. There'd been times when he'd searched for his father's face in his own reflection in the mirror. His mother's eyelids were drooping, and he tossed questions at her as if talking to himself; things he wanted to ask before becoming a father.

'What was my father like, Mum? Tell me. Was he ugly? Was he poor? Did you leave him because he was an asshole? Or was it something else?'

Did you love that guy, Mum? Is there someone you still can't forget? He shut his mouth tight before he could ask these last two questions. She could never know he'd read her diary.

'It's you I love,' Yuriko said languidly, answering his unspoken questions.

Who did she mean by 'you', Izumi wondered. His father? Asaba? Someone else? Someone Izumi didn't even know? As she lost her memories of love, who would be the last person she thought of at the end of her life?

'Can I really become a father?'

The question, locked deep inside, had slipped from Izumi's mouth.

For as long as he could remember, he'd never had a father. No man to look up to or depend on; no one to fear or hate. He and his mother had filled that gap together. But what then was a father – this baffling entity he was about to become?

What kind of man had his father been? The kind who would abandon a wife and child? If so, would Izumi be like that one day too? He had sought answers from his mother during that visit, but she'd sunk back into a daze.

'Yuriko, that custard looks delicious!'

Mizuki, the director, peered into Yuriko's face. As Izumi watched his mother's smile deepen, he thought once again how glad he was that she lived here. Nagisa Home's greatest attraction was the director herself; her strength and sunny disposition.

'Izumi's come to visit today, Yuriko. Would you like to play the piano?'

'She started playing piano again?' Izumi asked.

'Yes, and we're hoping she'll perform at the music recital we're planning next month.'

As Izumi digested this startling news, Kaori stepped in. 'That's wonderful,' she said, wiping the sweat from her brow. The room was a little warm for a pregnant woman. 'Our baby will be born by then. It would be great if we could all come together.'

A young staff member named Shunsuke led Yuriko to the piano. Bending over, he adjusted the height of the bench. He was darkly tanned and muscular with unruly hair and a strong accent. When asked, he'd told Izumi he came from an island called Amami Oshima near Okinawa. Although slightly scatterbrained, this hardworking young man who showered his boyish grin on everyone was a favourite of Izumi's mother. She'd eagerly told Izumi that Shunsuke was very good at the *sanshin*, a traditional Okinawan three-stringed instrument.

'How's she doing?' Izumi asked Mizuki, who stood beside him gazing at Yuriko. Last month, his mother had caught a cold and come down with a fever.

'She's completely recovered and emotionally stable too. She doesn't wander off either. Although really, almost no one at Nagisa Home does.'

'So even though you don't lock the doors, no one leaves.'

The doors and windows were left unlocked during the day. Subtle interior design features, such as a threshold or a slight difference in floor height, let residents know where they belonged. A group of elementary school students had visited recently, and the walls were covered with pictures they'd made with the residents.

Mizuki often said it was better for people to live all mixed together: adults and children, healthy people and patients, animals and even robots.

'We just try to make this a place where people feel comfortable staying.'

'Even so, haven't there been any residents who've wandered off and got lost?'

'Occasionally.' Mizuki's daughter, who had come up behind them without Izumi noticing, answered for her mother. 'When that happens, we all go looking together. Fortunately, it's a small town and people in the neighbourhood are very helpful. They call us right away to let us know where the person is or which direction they were headed. The whole town is kind of watching out for them. We're very grateful.'

Stroking her belly, Kaori said, 'My mother-in-law looks so much happier since she came here.'

'But,' Izumi said, his anxiety finding its voice. His eyes rested on Yuriko's back, now so thin. She tested the keyboard tentatively, pressing one note at a time while Shunsuke supported her. The piano emitted feeble, muffled sounds. Her figure was a far cry from the woman who had once played the grand piano so boldly. 'I'm glad she's healthy, but she seems to be losing her memory so fast. She's totally forgotten who my wife is, and these days I often can't understand what she's talking about. If I just go along with whatever she's says, it feels like I'm lying to her, and I find that really hard.'

'You find it painful to go along with what she says?' Mizuki asked.

With his eyes still fixed on Yuriko, Izumi said, 'It's like I'm making fun of her. Like I'm tricking a child.'

'I disagree,' Mizuki said. Startled by her emphatic tone, Izumi glanced towards her and found her dark eyes on him.

Yuriko began to play a piece. 'Ave Maria', by Gounod; that repetitive sacred melody. She played slowly, as though following a memory, seeking out the appropriate keys and pressing each one. Izumi recalled Yuriko telling him that when she played this piece she felt as though her fingertips were being scrutinised by a strict teacher.

'When my daughter was little, I used to go along with the things she said.' Mizuki shifted her eyes back to Yuriko. 'Everything from little discoveries to half-formed opinions, and at times, even the craziest fantasies. But it was fun. I felt like it expanded my world. Yuriko must have done the same for you. Wouldn't it be confining to always be stuck inside your own inner world?'

An elderly woman in a white silk blouse and royal-blue skirt, who had strolled over to the piano when Yuriko began playing, burst into song; a boisterous rendition of the folk song 'Aka Tombo' with full vibrato. The familiar melody filled the room without regard for the piano's tempo.

'*Red dragonfly, red dragonfly at sunset*
When was it I watched you while carried on my mother's back?'

Although the disparate melodies overlapped incongruously, Yuriko played with increasing passion, as if uplifted by the other woman's voice. She stumbled occasionally, but continued pressing the keys with her slender fingers. The habits she'd developed as a pianist seemed to be returning along with the music. The other resident, wide-eyed, continued to belt out the song.

'*In the mountain fields, the mountain fields*
We gathered mulberries, in baskets, in small baskets
Or was that just a dream?'

When the 'Ave Maria–Aka Tombo' jam session concluded, its muddy resonance lingering in the air, the elderly woman trotted towards Izumi, her royal blue skirt swirling. She caught him in a piercing gaze that seemed to say, 'I've found you.' Izumi, hands raised in applause, paused mid-clap and met her eyes.

'Are you happy?' she asked.

Although disconcerted by the abrupt question, Izumi responded with a feeble, 'Yes.'

'Before you is the opportunity to seize far greater happiness. The end of the world is nigh. God will choose His children and take them to the Promised Land. In that place, there's no regret, pain or sorrow. Only eternal happiness. Come, let us go together.'

As Izumi sat perplexed, Yuriko spoke up from behind the woman. 'Izumi, Mrs Minegishi always eats her strawberry first. How I envy her. I wish I could be like that.'

Mrs Minegishi turned to Yuriko. 'Are you happy?' she asked.

Yuriko smiled. 'Oh, yes. I'm watching the boats from here. I'm the happiest I've ever been.'

'You have a beautiful spirit. I can tell. Never-ending happiness will be yours in the Promised Land.'

'A thief broke in and took photo albums and pennants. He stole my memories.'

'Let us make a new world together. You will surely be chosen by God.'

'Izumi likes hayashi rice, you know. I'll make you some right away so that no one takes your pretty marbles. You just wait right there, okay?'

'Repent. God will forgive all your sins and shortcomings. God is great; God is magnanimous.'

To Izumi, their conversation seemed disjointed, each saying whatever happened to pop into her head. Yet they went on endlessly, nodding to each other throughout.

'Mrs Minegishi doesn't have any family to come and see her,' Mizuki's daughter said, as if guessing what Izumi was thinking. 'While busy with her religion, she got divorced, and her daughter, who joined the religion with her, decided to quit after graduating from senior high. When Mrs Minegishi came to us, she'd been living on her own for a long time. Perhaps God is all she has.'

I wonder if that's true, Izumi thought. Her ramblings seemed to show she'd retained only the outer husk of her faith. Or was it that her faith had simply changed shape, remaining alive in her heart even as her memory slipped away?

The residents and staff, as well as Izumi and Kaori, made dinner together and sat at the long wooden table to eat. Mackerel cooked in miso, *hijiki* seaweed stewed with soybeans, a salad made with fresh tomatoes from a nearby field and miso soup with mangetout . It was past eight when they finished, and the buzzing of the cicadas had died away. Beside him, Kaori stifled a yawn. Pregnant women near their due date got tired out early.

Mizuki and Yuriko accompanied Izumi and Kaori to the front entrance, where they stood waiting for a cab.

'Mum, I'm going to take some time off soon,' Izumi said. 'Let's go somewhere together.'

Yuriko always looked sad when it was time for Izumi to leave. Once, she'd even begged him not to go, saying he could stay there overnight. Since then, he'd always made a date to see her again before they said goodbye.

Mizuki smiled and took Yuriko by the arm. 'Yuriko, you're in good shape these days. Why don't you go on an outing with Izumi?' Mizuki kept her cheerfulness right into the evening, and Izumi couldn't help admiring her indefatigable stamina and attentiveness.

'Fireworks . . .' Yuriko murmured sleepily, perhaps tired from playing the piano earlier.

'Fireworks? That's a great idea. Why don't we go and see some?' Izumi responded before realising that Yuriko had been about to say more.

'Half fireworks.'

'Half? What do you mean?'

Yuriko frowned as if searching for the words to answer his question, but it seemed she couldn't find any that fit. Instead, she kept repeating 'half fireworks'. Their conversation was interrupted by the arrival of the taxi, gravel scrunching beneath its tires.

'Okay, Mum,' Izumi said. 'I'll look into fireworks for you.'

He turned and was about to get into the taxi when his mother stepped unsteadily forward and wrapped her arms around him.

'I love you,' she murmured into his ear. Her voice tremulous and low, was intimate, meant for him alone. The arms embracing him didn't feel like a mother's. Kaori watched them from inside the car. Embarrassed, Izumi pulled himself free and got into the taxi.

As the car sped along the edge of the dark sea, he recalled his mother's scent when she'd hugged him. Sweet like a flower, bitter like a weed. Suddenly, he remembered something she'd said when he was a boy and she'd held him in her arms on the futon. 'You smell just like your mummy.'

Having slept the whole way back in the train, Kaori was wide awake once they reached home. She opened her laptop on the dining table and began to work. Glancing through her emails, she groaned. There were over ten she needed to reply to.

'Sounds like a pretty heavy workload for a pregnant woman,' Izumi teased. While he worried about her, he spoke lightly on purpose. She'd been adamant about working until just before the baby was born, and he knew it helped take her mind off the pregnancy.

'Yeah, I know, but it was my decision to keep working on this project, so I need to do my part before I take maternity leave.'

The concerts she had booked for a German symphony orchestra were just two months away. Preparations for the album recording, which was planned to coincide with the orchestra's visit, as well as the production of posters and fliers, were all in the final stages. Izumi recalled what Maki had said. *You'll probably seek the same level of perfection in child-rearing as you do in your work.*

'Aren't people nervous when you come to meetings with such a big baby bump?'

Izumi opened a bottle of Perrier, which he bought by the case, poured it over ice in two glasses and placed one beside Kaori's laptop.

'Thanks.' She smiled up at him. 'It would actually be easier if they'd just be honest and tell me I don't need to come. I'd probably get more help that way too. But these days, I think people are afraid of being called sexist.'

'It's complicated, isn't it? It'd help if people would just decide which one is right.'

'It's out of the question to order a pregnant woman to work, but at the same time, some women might take being told not to work as discrimination. In the end, I guess it just depends on how each woman feels.'

As they spoke, Kaori kept tapping away at the keyboard and, in no time, had finished answering half her emails.

'I bet my mother worked right up until I was born. She was a single parent and her own parents seem to have disowned her. She checked herself into the hospital and gave birth on her own.'

The account of Izumi's birth, written in his mother's diary. He'd never heard that story from Yuriko herself.

'She must have felt so alone.'

'I know. I realise now how hard it must have been for her. To support me, she had to keep working even after she gave birth, plus do all the housework.'

Kaori nodded, then, as if she'd suddenly remembered something, she raised her eyes from the laptop. Izumi could hear the popping of the Perrier in their glasses.

'That reminds me. Your mother didn't touch her miso soup either.'

Izumi and Yuriko had been the only ones at dinner that night to not even taste the miso soup. They'd removed their bowls to the sink quickly so no one would notice, but it seemed they hadn't escaped Kaori's eyes.

The last time he'd eaten his mother's miso soup was on a spring day when it had snowed in the morning. After feeding Izumi his breakfast, his mother had left the house and not come back.

Izumi waited alone for five days. Some of her piano students came to the house, but not knowing what to say, he'd pretended he wasn't home. On the day all the food in the fridge and freezer was gone and he'd used up what little money his mother had left, he opened the notebook his mother had placed on the table and dialled his grandmother's number.

When she heard that her daughter had run off and left her son behind, his grandmother was speechless. Finally, she said, 'I'll be there by evening,' and told him to wait in the house until she arrived. Then she hung up. While waiting for his grandmother, Izumi took all the photos of him and Yuriko – the ones on the fridge, in frames, in albums, every single one he could find – and threw them in the rubbish bin.

His grandmother came about twice a week, but each time, she kept sighing, as if in protest at having been dragged into this mess against her will. She appeared to take care of Izumi only out of a sense of duty. And Izumi was sorry. He also thought it was pretty disgraceful for his mother to abandon him and run away when she was the one who'd decided to raise him on her own. He suspected his grandmother probably felt the same way about her daughter. He and his grandmother were bonded by his mother's disgrace.

One year later, Yuriko had returned as though nothing had happened and went straight to the kitchen.

Izumi woke to the aroma of miso soup. His mother was stirring a steaming pot in the kitchen. His grandmother sat limply on the sofa staring blankly at the morning news on the TV. She looked relieved rather than angry.

Izumi felt neither joy at his mother's return nor anger at her disappearance. Astonished, he merely said, 'Good morning.' 'Welcome home' might have been more appropriate. But instead, he'd chosen the words, 'Good morning.'

If they simply cut those twelve months from their life and spliced the ends together, like editing a film, that morning would look like a continuation of the same scene a year earlier. Izumi and Yuriko accepted this 'edit', making the tacit decision to carry on with their lives as though she'd never left.

They never mentioned it. For Izumi, life with his mother resumed unchanged. Except for one thing. He could not bring himself to eat the miso soup she made that morning. And Yuriko never touched her bowl either. From that day on, they both stopped eating miso soup.

After finding his mother's diaries, Izumi had kept them for a while in his desk at the office. He didn't want to see what had been cut from that spliced film. Occasionally, during a lull at work, he would take them out of the drawer and gaze at the two black covers: 1994 and 1995.

He finally realised he'd been hoping all this time that his mother would one day tell him about that year. He also realised that, having developed dementia, most likely she never would.

Late that night in the empty office, he'd read the diaries in one go. Unable to digest the content in just one reading, he read them several times. Scenes from the year Yuriko had tried to live without him rose vividly into his mind. The town where she'd lived, her little apartment, the *omurice* she loved, the goldfish, her friend Y, the man named Asaba. As well as everything that had happened on the day of the earthquake.

From the moment she returned to Izumi, his mother had dedicated all her time and her heart to her son. She showed no sign of being in love, and he thought she never questioned her choice to stay with him. Perhaps she'd resolved to spend the rest of her life atoning for her absence.

'Izumi! Look!'

Kaori's voice came from across the table. She beckoned him to the laptop, and he looked at the screen. She appeared to have finished responding to emails because the screen showed the results of a web search. The words 'half fireworks' had been typed into the search box, and an image of fireworks exploding above a lake was on the screen. A semicircular burst was reflected on the water's surface to form a full circle. The top half was real light. The bottom half, an illusion.

'They're beautiful,' Izumi breathed.

'Lake Suwa Fireworks Festival,' Kaori read aloud.

12

'Izumi, do you have a moment?' Nagai asked at the end of the regular Monday meeting.

'Yeah, sure. Want to talk here?' Izumi said, thinking they could stay in the meeting room. But when he glanced at the door, he saw four or five employees lined up outside, laptops in hand.

'Guess not. Looks like there's a queue,' Nagai said.

Izumi sighed. 'I wish they'd hurry up and solve this problem,' he said as they stepped out into the corridor. The company had a serious shortage of meeting rooms, and meeting dates and times were often determined by room availability.

'But that could be a good sign, you know.'

'What makes you say that?'

'I've heard newspaper companies have so few meetings these days that their meeting rooms are always empty.'

'So we're at least better off than that, huh?'

'That's right,' Nagai said. Slipping his phone from the pocket of his oversized hoodie, he began tapping the screen. 'But it's pretty messed up that the room schedule takes precedence over human schedules.'

The door to the lesson room at the end of the corridor opened and a teenager with black hair stepped out. He had a towel slung around his neck and was perspiring heavily. Izumi guessed he'd probably just finished a voice training session. Perhaps he was a new artist being trained by one of the company's labels. Though he was slight of build, an intense light shone from the eyes peering out beneath frizzy bangs.

'We could go to a coffee shop or something,' Izumi suggested, but Nagai said 'Here's fine,' and sank into a red sofa in the hallway.

When Izumi sat beside him, Nagai shot him a sly smile. 'Did you hear about Tanabe?' he said in a hushed tone.

'Has she broken up with Osawa?'

'Nope. They haven't split yet. But she's started going out with someone else at the same time. Someone who works at the company.'

'She picked someone that close? Does Osawa know?'

The dark-haired boy passed in front of them and disappeared into the toilets. Glancing at his profile as he went by, Izumi recognised him as a singer-songwriter who'd made a much-publicised major debut last month. His lyrics, which candidly described wrist cutting and other forms of self-harm, had caused quite a stir, and he'd leaped to stardom after a live performance in front of Shibuya Station attracted a crowd of over a thousand.

'I doubt Osawa knows. He seems like the jealous type, don't you think?'

'Tanabe's taking a big risk.'

'I suppose so, but it's so like her to want both guys at once. I guess I can empathise with that in some way. Still, you're always so out of the loop, aren't you, Izumi?'

Nagai grinned without taking his eyes off his phone. Izumi was both embarrassed by his own denseness and impressed with Nagai's ability to get the latest gossip. Where and when did he get hold of such intimate information?

'How's your mother?'

Izumi noticed Nagai's deep-set eyes were now trained on him. He couldn't tell from Nagai's expression whether he was just avoiding getting to the point he wanted to talk to Izumi about or whether he was actually concerned about Izumi's mother.

'She's doing okay. The nursing home's a good one, so that's great. But her dementia is progressing. She's already forgotten who Kaori is, and there are times when she doesn't know who I am either.'

'It's like they revert to being a child again, isn't it?'

It was true. Each time they met, Yuriko's words and behaviour seemed more childish. Perhaps her memories were flowing backwards.

'The other day, when I was leaving the home, she suddenly embraced me, as if she thought I was someone else.'

'Really? That must have been kind of awkward.'

'Yeah, exactly. It made me realise she's not just my mother, but a woman.' In his mind, he saw his mother sitting on a bench. Watching a white ship as she waited for Asaba. 'I never thought about her falling in love before, but being a mother is really only one side of her.'

'I know what you mean. My grandmother did some weird things too.' As Nagai spoke, the boy came out of the toilets. His sleeves were rolled up, exposing his arms. For someone who sang about self-harm, the skin on his wrists was fair and unscarred.

'Even though she knew her sons would fight over her inheritance, she didn't leave a will. She was warned repeatedly by her accountant and her lawyer to make one before she got dementia, but she refused to the very end. My dad and uncles couldn't believe how stubborn she was about it. But I can kind of guess why she did it.'

The boy's white arms sparked memories of KOE. Izumi saw her curled up on the sofa in the hotel room overlooking Shibuya when she had told him she'd forgotten music.

'I think it was Grandma's way to get their love. Her sons vied with each other to visit because she hadn't written a will. They'd come and ask her how she was, offer to get her anything she needed or to take her out somewhere. That's why she avoided making a decision. But in the end, she went senile and her sons had a huge fight over the inheritance. Everyone was trying to get back the love they'd given her.'

KOE had decided to switch to another company. Izumi had heard this the week before. Apparently, she was willing to sing anything, even other people's lyrics. After being so particular about using her own words.

'How can you create a human being?'

KOE's soft voice murmured in his ear.

Curious to see what she was doing, he'd searched the web and found a video of an interview between KOE and an up-and-coming AI expert.

'To make artificial intelligence is to create a human being,' the expert said in response to KOE's question. 'We have the computer memorise everything. If the AI is for *shogi*, we have it memorise the records of every *shogi* match in the past.'

'So what makes us human is our memories, not our bodies?'

KOE herself had been eager to do this interview, and her eyes shone with excitement.

'That's right,' the expert said. 'If I were injured in a bad car accident and my body was replaced by a machine, as long as my memories remained intact, you could say that person was me. But if I were to lose my memory, I would cease to be me, even if my body was unharmed.'

Was the person who'd forgotten how she'd written lyrics and with what feelings she'd sung them no longer KOE then? Izumi recalled her vacant eyes gazing down at the nightscape from her hotel.

Near the end of the interview, KOE said, as if to herself, 'If you wanted to give AI a personality or ability, I guess you could have it forget something then. Such as the colour red, or the sea, or love.'

Perhaps she's right, Izumi thought. What makes a person unique may come from the things they lack. Pictures painted by an artist with no memory of red or stories created by a writer with no memory of love would still be attractive. KOE had lost her memory of music. What had she gained in its place? He'd like to hear music by her again.

'So, you're going to quit after all?' The words slipped from his mouth before he realised it.

'I'm sorry Izumi.' Nagai shoved his phone back in his pocket.

'You said you'd do your best to fill in for me.'

'I've made my decision. I thought I should tell you myself.'

Izumi smiled wryly. 'Did you have to pick a sofa in the corridor for such an important announcement?'

Nagai returned his smile. 'It's not such a big deal that I need to tell you formally in a meeting room, you know.'

Osawa had told Izumi yesterday that Nagai wanted to quit. He'd given Osawa the standard excuse of having found something else he wanted to do, but Izumi found that hard to accept. Nagai was just at the point where his work would get more interesting.

'You don't remember anything, do you?' Nagai said as if reading Izumi's thoughts. 'I told you before. What I really want to do is film.'

Sifting through his memory, Izumi realised that Nagai probably had told him. He remembered Nagai saying he liked movies better than music, but Izumi hadn't taken him seriously, assuming it was just sarcasm.

'Someone from a film company liked the Ongaku video and invited me to join them. He said there aren't enough film producers.'

'You can make animation and small-scale movies with us too, you know.'

'I know. But I want to give this a shot. To make the kind of movies that even my family out in the sticks can see, the kind shown at cinema complexes. I'd like to see my name on the end roll. I realise it's stupid, but I feel like that way I won't be forgotten.'

The black-haired youth had disappeared from the hallway. Izumi heard the lively strains of guitar and drums from the lesson room, but their brightness didn't seem to fit the artist.

'All right. I'll talk with Osawa about handing over your job.'

'Thank you.' Nagai took off his cap with its straight visor and bowed his head. 'I doubt he'll be disappointed to see me go. I don't think he liked me much.'

'That's not true. I told you when you first came here. It wasn't me but Osawa who wanted you to join us.'

Nagai's eyes wavered slightly at this. 'Really? I'd totally forgotten,' he murmured. Putting on his cap, he pulled the visor down over his eyes.

Kaori and Izumi dropped by a shop selling baby goods on their way back from Kaori's check-up. She was in her last month of pregnancy, and her movements seemed ponderous. Izumi had offered to buy what they needed and bring it home, but Kaori said she wanted a walk.

Disposable nappies, thick bum wipes, plastic bibs, spoons for baby food. They thought they had stocked up on everything they needed, but when they looked at the shelves in the store, they realised there was still a lot they'd forgotten. They checked the merchandise methodically, consulting as they went along to make sure they got everything they needed. After they'd done a full circuit, the items in his shopping basket reminded Izumi of the nursing care goods he'd recently bought for his mother.

Perhaps because it was a Saturday, there was a long queue at the till. Glancing around, Izumi realised that only certain types of customers came here: those who were expecting a baby and those who had small children. Most were couples, and there was an air of bubbly anticipation.

'To be honest . . . I didn't feel happy when I found out I was pregnant.'

It took Izumi a few moments to realise the voice he'd heard was Kaori's. She stood beside him, clutching a pack of disposable nappies with both hands.

'I wondered if I'd be able to keep working. I was pissed off that I'd have to stop drinking for a while and travelling overseas. I couldn't stop dwelling on things like that.'

Izumi heard a thin wail. 'Mama.' A little girl who looked to be only one or two years old seemed to be lost in the toy corner on their right. Her pink sandals pattered against the floor as she walked unsteadily.

'It frustrated me that I'd have to take time off work too. I've accomplished so much over the years, made so many connections and work was just starting to get interesting. I worried that someone might take over my job while I was away. I resented you sometimes, you know. It seems so unfair that men don't have to give up anything when they have a baby. But you didn't feel happy about the pregnancy either, right?'

Caught off guard, Izumi couldn't think of anything to say. He remembered feeling numb when she'd told him she was pregnant. He'd felt no joy or excitement, and it was all he could do to say, 'That's great.' Kaori had teased him, saying he sounded as if it had nothing to do with him, but her smile reached only the corners of her mouth.

'Actually, I was relieved by your reaction. I thought, "I guess we can become parents together." You probably think you're hiding your feelings well, but what you think is written all over your face. Which means I never feel uncertain about you. I need that kind of reassurance. I never understood what my parents were thinking and was always trying to guess from their expressions.'

Kaori was looking straight ahead, her gaze fixed on the front of the queue where the till emitted regular digital beeps.

In the lobby of the maternity ward, looking at the other couples sitting on the sofas, Izumi had suddenly wanted to ask each one, 'Why did you decide to have a baby? Are you happy about becoming a parent?'

'I went to visit Maki right after their baby was born. I wanted to hear all about it. I was hoping she'd say the baby was so adorable it made her forget all the pain and suffering. But instead, she said having a baby means giving up everything. Time, money, energy, knowledge – the baby takes it all.'

The pleas of the little girl wearing pink sandals were growing damper by the minute. She kept calling, 'Mama, Mama!' while tears streamed unheeded down her cheeks. Izumi looked around, wondering where her mother was, but he couldn't see any likely candidate. Kaori kept talking as if she hadn't noticed.

'I was so disappointed. Everything she said confirmed my worst fears.'

'I see . . .'

'But, you know, when Maki began nursing her baby, she looked transformed. Like she'd become an adult. And that made me think: maybe we need to lose something if we want to grow up.' Saying no more, Kaori placed the package of nappies on the floor and hurried over to the little girl. She patted her head hesitantly, but the girl kept crying. Kaori stared at her for a moment, as though considering what to do, then took a deep breath and shouted, 'Mum! Where are you? Your little girl's lost!' But no mother came running. Kaori beckoned to Izumi.

'Put her on your shoulders!' she shouted.

'Huh? But I don't know how.'

'Just do it! Quick!'

Kaori's order unsettled Izumi. He'd never given anyone a shoulder ride before, and no one had ever given him one either. Drawing on memories of things he'd seen on TV, he slipped his hands under the girl's armpits and raised her over his head and onto his shoulders. Though small, she was quite heavy and wobbled precariously. Izumi grabbed her thin little legs to steady her. Her pink sandals dangled from her toes, swaying in front of him.

The little girl, who had no way of knowing that this was the first shoulder ride Izumi had ever given in his life, stopped crying abruptly, as if taken by surprise. 'Mum! Where are you!' Kaori's voice reverberated through the shop; a cry such as Izumi had never heard from her before. It made her seem like a different person.

He heard footsteps behind him. A woman pushing a pram with a shopping bag in it rushed up and took the little girl from Izumi's shoulders. She pressed her cheek tightly against her daughter's forehead and bowed repeatedly to Kaori and Izumi.

Izumi watched the pink sandals swaying from the girl's toes. Where, he wondered, was his mother going, leaving everything behind, her stuff, her words, her memories. Maybe we need to lose something if we want to grow up. Kaori's words echoed in his ears for a long time.

13

The golden light of the evening sun struck Izumi as he stepped from the covered shopping avenue into the main street. Joining the throng of people, all of whom were reduced to dark shadows, he gripped his mother's hand and moved forward slowly, very slowly.

Three young women dressed in light summer yukata – one red, one indigo and one yellow – darted through a gap in the crowd and ran ahead, their wooden *geta* clacking against the pavement. Yuriko, who wore a more subdued white yukata, stared after them with a smile. 'How pretty,' she said.

Stalls were being erected along both sides of the curved street. Sweat-drenched owners pulled awnings tight, adjusted propane tanks and placed iron griddles over burners. Some stalls were ready to open, while others didn't have their frames up yet, but all the stall keepers looked eager to get started. Seating areas on the roofs of hotels around the lake were already jammed with spectators.

The sound of drumming came from somewhere. Up above, the sky was a greyish-blue, and jutting into it were the necks of two large construction cranes topped with lights that illuminated the seating areas. A first aid tent had been set up between the bases of the cranes, and several patients had been brought in, even though the fireworks hadn't started yet.

Ahead, Izumi saw the entrance to the stands where he'd reserved seats. Holding his mother's hand, he helped her up the steps, one by one. They'd walked nearly twenty minutes from the hotel, and she was out of breath. Although he'd suggested she use a wheelchair, she'd said she wanted to walk with him. He'd complied, thinking they wouldn't have many chances to walk together again.

When they finally reached the top of the stands, the oval-shaped lake spread before them. Dark blue waves lapped gently against the shore. On the floating island from which the fireworks would be launched was a Shinto *torii* gate; it gave the impression some ancient ritual was about to be performed. Spectators clustered along the edge of the lake, hugging the shoreline, while the dark mountains on the far shore gazed down upon the huge crowd.

Sitting beside his mother in the stands, which were divided into sections by white nylon string, Izumi watched the surface of the lake change from deep blue to black. At seven o'clock sharp, a voice announced the start of the festival, followed by a burst of red fireworks. Explosions thundered, one after another.

Viewed up close, the fireworks were far more impressive than Izumi had imagined. A gasp escaped his lips, just as his mother gasped beside him. Hearing their voices overlap, she glanced at him and smiled. Her eyes held the intimacy of a lover, as if to say, 'You feel just like I do, don't you?'

Multiple heart-shaped fireworks burst overhead to the strains of a ballad that had topped the hit chart earlier that year, and a cheer rose from the crowd. Next came showers of stars that covered the sky in sync with the soundtrack from a popular sci-fi movie. Fireworks displays followed one after the other, forming shapes Izumi had never seen. UFOs, butterflies, snails, four-leafed clover. After each one, the spectators around him picked up their pens and wrote numbers into a booklet.

Yuriko was staring with curiosity at a young man with bleached hair sitting next to her. He showed her his booklet. 'The fireworks festival's a competition,' he explained. 'This column here's for scoring.' He grinned, exposing gold-capped teeth. His black yukata was embroidered with a dragon and had indecipherable Chinese characters printed right down to the hem. Beside him, his girlfriend wore one with the same dragon pattern, and her brown hair was piled on top of her head.

'The competitors are from all over Japan. That last one was from Ibaraki and the next is from Nagano,' the young man went on. 'Then there'll be one from Akita, followed by Niigata. There's an entry from Tokyo too.'

As each elaborate display shot up into the sky, the MC announced the name of the company that manufactured them. The young man's girlfriend greeted them all with shrieks of 'Cool!' 'Amazing!' or 'Wow! I like that one!' and wrote a number in her booklet.

'You've gone and given them all a hundred,' the young man teased her. Turning to Yuriko, he said, 'Hey, lady. Why don't you give it a go? The judges' scores will be in tomorrow's paper, and it's fun to check them against your own.' He thrust his pen and booklet at Yuriko. 'Go ahead, I'll share with her,' he said, nodding to his girlfriend.

Although she looked taken aback at first, Yūriko smiled and thanked him. 'I'm okay,' she said.

'If you're worried about us, don't be. We don't mind. Come on. Give it a try!'

The young man pushed the booklet at them so insistently that Izumi finally took it. Opening it, he saw a list of titles for every entry. Yuriko peered at the words for some time, then said, 'I forget everything, you know. I can't remember which fireworks were good, what colour they were, or what shape. But I think that's why they're so beautiful.' She took the booklet from Izumi and handed it back to the young man.

Thinking his mother might have offended him, Izumi ducked his head in apology, but the man exclaimed, 'You know, you're right! That's quite profound!' He and his girlfriend looked at each other and nodded vigorously, their multiple earrings jiggling. Meanwhile, the fireworks continued to burst and fade.

These days, his mother no longer called him 'Izumi'. Although she still recognised him as her son, she seemed to have difficulty remembering what to call him. She was losing even the name she'd uttered thousands or tens of thousands of times.

She'd also begun sleeping more, as if in proportion to the amount of vocabulary she was losing. Often, she curled up on her bed from the early afternoon and stayed there without budging. The hours she napped were gradually increasing. Izumi recalled her baby-like face as she slept in a pool of sunlight. What of him would remain with her once she'd lost all her words and forgotten his name completely?

When the pyrotechnic displays of all twenty-five contestants were done, darkness engulfed the sky. Score sheet completed, the bleached-haired young man drained his can of beer and pronounced that year's exhibition 'Awesome!' Yuriko clutched her unopened bottle of tea in both hands and stared fixedly at the ripples on the black surface of the lake.

'And now for the grand finale!' the MC announced, her voice shrill. 'Suwa Lake's famed Star Mine on the Water!' A huge semicircle of light burst before their eyes. There was a short pause, then a low, heavy noise, like the earth rumbling, resounded across the water. A cheer rose from the audience. In rapid succession, more semicircles of light burst just above the water and were reflected on its mirror-like surface. The arches in the sky united with their reflections in the water to depict full circles.

'What a climax!' exclaimed the MC. 'Like a hundred flowers blooming!'

Watching the semicircles of light floating on the water, images rose in Izumi's mind. The myriad flowers displayed in the single-flower vase of their little house. Tulips, cosmos, hydrangeas, sunflowers, gerberas, marguerites, camellias, roses, rapeseed blossoms. Their colours withering and fading away unnoticed, leaving only the memory of their beauty.

The fireworks flashed, casting white, red, and yellow lights across his mother's pale face as she gazed up with tears in her eyes. Izumi was suddenly sure he'd witnessed a similar scene somewhere before. An infinitely precious scene. Words that must never be forgotten. But when? He searched his memory, yet no matter how hard he tried, he couldn't remember.

Swept along by the crowd, Izumi grasped his mother's hand.

'Those fireworks were so pretty, weren't they?' he said.

'I want a candy apple,' said a little-girl voice from behind him, and he felt a tug on his hand. Turning, he saw Yuriko gazing at a little stall jammed between one selling shaved ice and another offering yo-yo fishing. A bright red apple adorned the stall's indigo curtain. Candy apples on sticks were lined up in a row in a base of Styrofoam, the candy coating on their surfaces glistening under the light-bulb. They looked so much like glasswork, Izumi found it hard to believe they were food.

'I'm tired. I want a candy apple right now.'

Watching her mouth move, Izumi realised that the girlish voice he'd heard belonged to his mother. The childish tone was so different from when they were watching the fire-works display that it threw him off balance.

'There're too many people here. Let's get one a little later,' he said, and pulled her hand. He wanted to get out of the crowd and back to their room in the lakeside hotel as soon as possible.

'But I want one now.' Yuriko stopped and wouldn't budge, even at Izumi's urging. 'I want a candy apple. I want one now. I want one now.'

She repeated this over and over, like a spoiled child. Passersby dressed in yukata gave her curious looks. Embar-rassed, Izumi brought his mouth close to her ear and spoke soothingly. 'Okay, Mum. Let's go get one together.'

'I'll wait here.'

Izumi was hesitant to leave her on her own, but he could also see it would be difficult to get her across the press of people to the booth. 'All right. I'll go get one. You wait here. Don't move, okay?'

He sat his mother down on the curb and waded through the crowd as though swimming against the current. He was jabbed by people's shoulders and elbows, and someone clicked their tongue in disgust. Although this annoyed him, he suppressed his irritation. After all, he was the one causing the trouble. He had to get a candy apple and return to Yuriko as soon as possible. He kept looking over his shoulder to make sure she was still there.

By the time he finally reached the stall, he was dripping with sweat. 'Three hundred yen for one,' the stall owner said, casting the harassed-looking Izumi a suspicious glance. Izumi ordered one, thinking that was enough, but then changed his mind and got two so he could keep his mother company. He handed the man a 1,000 yen note and, after grabbing two apples on sticks and the change, turned round to find his mother gone. He stood on tiptoe and scanned the curb where she'd been sitting, but she was nowhere in sight.

A faint sigh escaped his lips. He should have insisted on bringing her with him to the stall. Or maybe he shouldn't have listened to her in the first place and instead taken her back to the hotel. But there was no point wasting time chiding himself for things he hadn't done; he had to look for her. Rallying himself, he squeezed his body back into the flow of people.

'Mum!' he shouted, standing tall and craning to see, but his voice was drowned out by the bustling crowd. Shadowy heads jostled like waves clashing in the darkness. His mother was so short, she'd disappear beneath those waves. 'Mum! Raise your hand!' He couldn't keep from crying out, even though he knew there'd be no answer.

Dark eyes turned to glare at him, annoyed by this stranger who'd suddenly started shouting. I must look ridiculous, Izumi thought. A grown man calling for his mother, a candy apple clutched in each hand. He wanted to chuck the apples, but couldn't bring himself to do so and hung on to them instead as he broke into a run and pushed his way through the crowd.

He ducked into every building along the street. A convenience store, a karaoke place, a buckwheat noodle shop, and several souvenir shops. But he couldn't find his mother anywhere.

He accosted shop staff, demanding to know if they'd seen a short woman, about seventy years old, wearing a white yukata, but they all shook their heads. It suddenly occurred to him that she might have returned to the hotel on her own, and he hurried back. Dashing into the lobby, he ran around asking every staff member he passed, but no one had seen Yuriko.

A shrill siren wove its way around to the front of the hotel, and a white vehicle passed down the road. Filled with foreboding, Izumi ran back to the entrance. Too impatient to wait for the automatic doors to open all the way, he angled his body sideways through them and raced after the ambulance's whirling red light. Like the sea parting for Moses in *The Ten Commandments*, the crowd pulled aside for the ambulance, revealing the road ahead.

The siren stopped in front of the first aid tent, and the rear door of the ambulance opened. The rescue team climbed out with a stretcher and entered the tent. As the plastic flap parted, Izumi glimpsed the slender legs of someone lying on a bed. 'Mum!' he yelled and hurried inside, but the patient was a teenage girl wearing a high-school uniform. The rescue team stared at Izumi with startled expressions. Flustered, he turned and fled outside, then ran aimlessly down the road where only a few stragglers remained.

Where could his mother have gone? He'd told her not to move! His wooden *geta* clattered dryly on the pavement.

When Izumi was seventeen, he had an older girlfriend, a university student. He met her at his part-time job. She'd come to Tokyo from Shikoku and lived on her own in an apartment two stations away.

'You're so cute, Izumi. Why don't you come over to my place?' She invited him over one day after work when they had dinner together. At her place, he drank alcohol for the first time in his life and, in the spur of the moment, had sex. 'You might as well stay the night,' she said, and he did as she suggested.

When he returned home at about noon the next day, all Yuriko said was, 'Welcome back.' She didn't reprimand him. She couldn't, and he knew that. For a while, he spent a lot of time with his girlfriend. Often, he didn't return home for three or four days.

About six months after they began seeing each other, he stayed with her for a whole week. When he came home, Yuriko finally asked, 'Where've you been? Who are you staying with?'

It was as if Izumi had been waiting for this moment. The words he'd saved up slid from his mouth. 'Are you serious? You have no right to say anything.'

His mother remained silent for some time, staring into the sink. When Izumi sat on the sofa and turned on the TV, she began moving her hands again, washing the dishes. 'I guess not,' she muttered.

The following week, Izumi broke up with the college girl.

There was a squeal of brakes, and Izumi turned. Headlights bore down on him, and he fell on his bottom, his hands thrust out in front of him. A shiny silver bumper stopped right at his fingertips. Two candy apples lay crushed on the ground, gleaming in the headlights. Izumi heard someone bellow, 'Idiot!' followed by the screech of wheels skidding on asphalt as the car backed up, then swerved round Izumi and sped away. His mind froze, and he smelled burning rubber. For a moment, he sat slumped on the ground unable to move.

A week earlier, Mrs Minegishi at Nagisa Home had passed away. She'd kept proselytising right up to her last breath. 'Believe in God,' she'd urged. 'If you do, you'll gain eternal life.'

Nagisa Home had hosted a small memorial. 'Even the solitary Mrs Minegishi once had a daughter who came to visit her occasionally,' Mizuki told Izumi. But those visits had ended abruptly. Wondering what happened, Mizuki contacted Mrs Minegishi's daughter and discovered that she'd been killed in a car accident. By then, Mrs Minegishi didn't even remember she had a daughter, but after her daughter stopped coming, she began preaching even more earnestly.

Staring at the taillights receding into the distance, Izumi realised that if he died now, there would be no one to remember his mother. Who would know that she rubs the tip of her nose when she's happy? Or that she loves custard pudding with the caramel sauce slightly burned, and placing a single white flower in a vase? If I die, Izumi thought, the person who knows these things will be gone. And when my mother goes, she'll die not only in reality but in memory too. This seemed incredibly sad, yet in the end, unless you happened to be a famous historical figure, that was everyone's fate.

Stall keepers began turning out their shop lights. Izumi ran along the road, weaving from one side to the other, in search of Yuriko. As the darkness spread, the lakeside emptied. Izumi was gasping for breath, and his throat was parched. Sweat rolled from his forehead into his eyes, and he staggered to a stop to wipe his brow with the sleeve of his yukata. He could feel his heart valves open and close rapidly in his chest. There was a burning sensation between his toes and, glancing down, he saw that the thong of his *geta*, which he hardly ever wore, had rubbed away the skin between his big and second toe. As he watched the blood well to the surface, a searing pain reached his brain. 'Ow!' he yelped, kicking off the wooden sandals.

'You always make such a big fuss about nothing.' His mother's words. She'd often said that to him when he was a boy. Thinking he heard her gentle voice behind him, he turned and saw her standing in a square lined with stalls. Goldfish scooping, a shooting gallery, yakisoba noodles, candyfloss, yo-yo fishing. The last cluster of stalls with their lights still on. People flocked to them like bugs to a light trap.

Yuriko was standing in front of a shaved ice shop, staring at a row of colourful syrups. Like a little girl trying to choose, her eyes shifted from red to green, blue and yellow.

'Mum!' Izumi shoved the *geta* back onto his feet and limped over to her.

Yuriko turned to look at him. 'Where were you?' she said. 'I've been looking all over for you.' She didn't look like she'd moved a single step from where he'd left her. There wasn't a drop of perspiration on her face, and her yukata wasn't the least bit rumpled. 'I was really worried, you know,' she said. 'Because you always get lost.'

'You're the one who got lost, Mum.' The words escaped him like a sigh. His pulse was still beating wildly, pounding against his eardrums inside his head.

'Remember when I took you to the amusement park? You got lost right away. You were gone when I came out of the toilets. You always did that. Just disappeared as soon as I took my eyes off you. And I searched all over for you, every time. But I knew what you were doing. You got lost because you wanted me to look for you, didn't you?'

Yuriko took Izumi's hand, entwining her fingers in his. In the past, it was Izumi who'd got lost. Now, it was his mother. In this way, they continued to confirm their relationship, testing their love for one another as parent and child.

'Do you remember the day we moved into the house? Our luggage didn't arrive.' Yuriko pointed a pale finger at the strawberry syrup. Izumi ordered one and paid 300 yen. The shopkeeper cranked the handle of the machine, and transparent slivers of ice piled up like snow in the paper cup.

'Really?'

'The movers made a mistake and delivered our stuff to a different customer. We were at our wits' end in that empty old house.'

They'd moved during the summer when Izumi was in junior high. Not long after his mother had returned from her year away. But his memory of that time was vague, and he couldn't recall it clearly.

The shopkeeper handed him a white mound of shaved ice in a paper cup. Bottles of colourful syrups lined the counter. Each had a spout so customers could freely choose the one they wanted. Izumi pressed the button for the strawberry syrup, turning the fluffy white ice bright red.

'We didn't have any furniture or dishes, so we ate at a soba noodle shop and bought watermelon at the green grocer in the shopping arcade. We got him to slice it for us, then ate it together on the little porch under the eaves. Remember?'

She described how they'd washed the floors of the empty rooms with rags, then walked down the hill in the dark. She'd ordered buckwheat noodles topped with deep-fried tofu and Izumi had ordered a set meal of chicken and eggs on rice with a small bowl of noodles. They'd watched a baseball game on the shop's TV while they ate. The green-grocer had sliced the big watermelon for them, and they'd devoured it side by side on the porch under the eaves while watching the lights go on in the apartment complex, the one that looked like it was made from Lego blocks.

As his mother's description became more detailed, a scene from that day came back.

'Mum, the movers haven't come yet.'

'I'm sorry, Izumi. I'm sure they'll get here sometime today.'

'That's okay, Mum.'

'This watermelon sure tastes good, doesn't it?'

'Mmm, great.'

'Izumi, I'm sorry you had to change schools because of the move.'

Ever since his mother had come back, she'd been apologising for everything. Sorry you have to wear cheap clothes. Sorry you have to eat readymade food from the deli. Sorry I can't take you on any trips.

'It's all right.'

'I hope you'll make lots of friends at your new school.'

'I'll be fine, Mum. I never had that many friends anyway.'

Still standing, Yuriko took a spoonful of the strawberry-flavoured ice. Her face screwed up at the first bite. 'It's cold,' she said. She scooped up another spoonful and shoved it towards Izumi's mouth, saying, 'It's good.' He took the bite she offered. The sweet scent of strawberry syrup rose up inside his nose along with the coldness of the ice.

'I want to see the half fireworks,' Yuriko murmured as she took another spoonful.

'Huh?' Thinking he'd misheard her, Izumi brought his face closer to hers.

'I want to see the half fireworks,' she repeated. There'd been no mistake.

'Mum, we just saw them.'

'No, not those. The half fireworks. I want to see them.'

'Mum, what're you talking about? They're the ones we just saw. I'm sure of it.'

'No. They're different. I want to see the half fireworks with you!'

The shopkeepers shot perplexed looks their way, as if caught up in an improv theatre performance. Like the fireworks reflected in the lake, the boundary between reality and fantasy in his mother's mind was beginning to blur. The shaved ice in her cup was rapidly melting into red liquid.

'Mum, please. Get hold of yourself.'

'But I want to see the half fireworks! Half fireworks. I want to see them!'

'Stop it, Mum!' Izumi shouted before he could stop himself. The cup of shaved ice fell from Yuriko's hand and landed at her feet. The cold liquid sprayed from the cup, and red stains spread across her white yukata. With trembling hands, she grabbed Izumi's arm. Her fingers dug into his skin as if trying to cling on to the memories she was losing.

'I can't find my stuffy . . . A little brown bunny. It's cute and soft. Maybe I dropped it somewhere . . . Grandma bought it for me.'

Her voice had become childish, and she began wandering back and forth, pulling Izumi along by the arm. She walked unsteadily, stumbling frequently, like a toddler that had only recently learned to walk.

'Its name is Moochan. I've been looking all over for it, but I can't find it anywhere. Mummy will be mad at me. You're nice . . . You'll help me find it, won't you?'

She stopped talking abruptly and peered at Izumi's face.

'Who are you?' she asked.

'Mum, it's me. Izumi.'

He couldn't meet her eyes. He didn't want to acknowledge what was happening. But Yuriko brought her face even closer to his and asked again, 'Who? Who are you?'

Who am I? he wondered. How could he explain? My name is Izumi Kasai. I'm your son. I'm a thirty-seven-year-old man. I work for a record company. My favourite food is hayashi rice. I like egg dishes too. I don't like miso soup. I married a colleague from the company, and our baby will be born soon.

But would any of this prove who he was?

'Who . . . are you? What am I doing here?'

Her questions reminded him of the memos he'd found scrawled on scraps of paper in her house. Had she been asking herself over and over 'Who am I?' just like he'd done now?

Her jet-black eyes shone like marbles in the light of the bulb hanging from the stall. What did those bottomless black eyes see when they looked at him?

Slowly, Yuriko gazed around at all the people. Looking into her innocent, childlike eyes, Izumi knew: she'd reverted completely. For infants, everyone they meet is an unknown face. So too for his mother, everyone was now a stranger.

14

Dolphins, sea turtles, jellyfish, squid. Sea creatures swam across an entire wall of Nagisa Home. Sketches made by residents on a visit to a nearby aquarium with a group of school children the previous Saturday. Done in pencil and crayon, the bright, multicoloured drawings made Izumi feel he was in some tropical sea.

The new resident who had moved in after Mrs Minegishi was short-tempered and often yelled at the staff. A former designer, the only thing that kept him calm and quiet was drawing, and the director, Mizuki, had come up with the idea of starting regular sketching sessions. Nagisa Home basically adjusted the rules to accommodate the most difficult residents.

The afternoon sun shone on the tropical seascape. The residents had gathered in the main room and were seated around the piano. As Yuriko made her way slowly through the audience, someone began to applaud. Mizuki's daughter and the helper, Shunsuke, supported her on either side. Yuriko was dressed in a neatly ironed white blouse and a lemon-yellow cardigan. Her eyes were fixed straight ahead on the upright piano. She didn't seem to notice Izumi. Lowering herself cautiously onto the piano bench, she stroked the keys with her fingers as though testing how they felt.

The first chord rang through the room.

Izumi could feel the residents holding their breath as they waited for the next note. Mizuki, who was standing beside the piano, clasped her hands as if in prayer, her gaze focused on his mother's profile.

Yuriko played one note, then another. But her fingers faltered and the melody came to a halt. She tried again, then a second and a third time, but each time the notes became jumbled and she couldn't go on. She shook her head as if telling herself, 'That's not right.'

She breathed a small sigh that seemed to announce she was going to start fresh and went back to the beginning. Slowly, meticulously, she placed one note on top of the other, and gradually the shape of the piece emerged. 'Träumerei', Movement No. 7 from Schumann's *Kinderszenen*. The melody Izumi had heard her play so many times in that little house. Despite the uneven tempo, the notes gradually came together, and the dreamlike refrain resonated in his ears. Sometimes you seem like a child. He recalled the words Clara had written to Schumann which he'd read in his mother's diary. A lump caught in his throat.

The four-bar melody rose and fell, increasing in complexity as it repeated. Yuriko missed several notes in a row. Like an avalanche, the sounds collapsed into a cacophony. Yuriko stared at her fingertips and tilted her head, as though to cover her embarrassment. Sweat spread across her back.

'What's she doing?' a boy piped up. He sat perched on his mother's lap, probably the grandson of a resident. His mother hastily covered his mouth with her hand but that didn't stop him. 'Can't she play properly?'

Yuriko readjusted herself on the bench and began again, but the little boy's voice grew louder, drowning out the piano. 'She did it again. Doesn't she know how to play?'

Yuriko sat staring at the keyboard, then rose soundlessly and buried her face in her hands. Her back, damp with perspiration, trembled, perhaps with frustration, or maybe with shame. Izumi couldn't bear to watch. He wanted to scream, 'Let her stop!', but Mizuki kept her eyes fixed on Yuriko's profile as if she still believed in something. Izumi recalled her telling him beforehand that no one would step in to help Yuriko at this recital. 'We want to hear her perform just as she is now,' she'd said.

A silence stole over the room. The hiss of waves could be heard from outside. Yuriko turned to look out the window, and the piano bench scraped dully against the floor. Her gaze rested on the waves lapping the shore. She stood motionless, like a doll, staring at the deep-blue sea.

'You can play as slowly as you like, but just try playing it through without stopping.'

Izumi's mother had told him this repeatedly when she taught him piano. *Play as slowly as you like, Mum.* With this refrain running through his mind, Izumi kept his eyes on her gaunt profile.

In the hushed room, the ebb and flow of the waves against the shore set a steady rhythm like a metronome. Yuriko sat down suddenly, as though she'd been freed. Her shoulders swayed in sync with the sound of the waves. Four-four time. Just as he'd done countless times as a child, Izumi watched his mother's back. Swaying to the metronome in front of the piano, keeping time.

She took a deep breath. Spreading her fingers across the keys, she pressed down firmly. The sound, much louder than anything she'd played before, bounced off the ceiling and into Izumi's ears.

'Stay true to the score. Don't ad lib or rearrange.'

Izumi could hear his mother's voice saying these words to the children she taught. His mother's fingers chased the keys earnestly. Rather than her memory of the score, it seemed as if her life itself was weaving the tune. A disciplined, orderly performance. Yet it held a hidden strength.

His mother bent over the keyboard, her back so much smaller now. She faced the piano with every ounce of strength in her small frame. Gradually, her fingers picked up speed. The notes glided together like a boat setting off into the sea.

She's leaving me for good, Izumi thought. He closed his eyes involuntarily. His long journey with his mother was coming to a close. As he listened to her play 'Träumerei', he saw her rowing out to sea. It was time to part. His nose stung inside. He took a deep breath.

The air smelled of flowers.

The fragrance triggered another image.

The day his mother had returned from Kobe, she'd sat alone at the piano and played 'Träumerei'. There was a single lily in the vase on the table, and its heady perfume wafted through the room. Bathed in the orange light of the setting sun that slanted through the window, his mother had swayed in time to the melody as though lost in some long dream.

When Kaori had been wheeled into the delivery room, leaving him behind on a bench in the lobby, Izumi had been overcome with unbearable anxiety. What if she vanished, leaving just him and their child? How would he carry on? It made sense he felt no maternal feeling, but he couldn't find the least speck of paternal feeling inside himself either. How could someone like him possibly become a parent?

Several deliveries appeared to be happening simultaneously. Nurses rushed back and forth, and doors burst open and slammed shut again. The tranquil synthesiser music on the speakers seemed at odds with all the commotion.

The day Izumi had realised in a crowded barbecue restaurant that he would one day marry Kaori, she'd told him she wanted to be a father to KOE. Perhaps he'd been hoping she'd supply the paternal instinct he knew he lacked. But as she was wheeled into the delivery room, grimacing in pain, she'd made no attempt to hide her fear.

'I think Yuriko wasn't sure of how to be a mother either.'

Kaori had made this remark as she and Izumi left their last prenatal check-up. In Izumi's eyes, Yuriko had been a mother from the very beginning. When they were together, he'd never sensed that she had any doubts or ambivalence. But sitting on the bench in this waiting room, he felt for the first time the shuddering anxiety, the loneliness Yuriko must have experienced when she went to the maternity clinic all on her own.

How long he waited, he didn't know, but a nurse finally called him, and he followed her into the delivery room. Within the feverish intensity of that space, the newborn baby, its body flushed crimson, was being bathed in warm water. Its limbs were curled up, and its voice was still so faint it could hardly be called a cry. He could tell from Kaori's ashen face that the birth had been traumatic. Even so, she smiled at Izumi. Her expression, like that of someone who had successfully completed a major job, was so like her.

A nurse handed Izumi the baby, washed and wrapped in a white towel. It smelled like new grass, the bittersweet smell of life. Its body was soft and delicate, as if the slightest pressure might crush it. Izumi touched its pink, twig-like fingers.

The baby grasped Izumi's index finger in its fist, squeezing it with a strength Izumi could never have imagined from such a tiny body, and began to cry loudly. At the sound of its wails, which shook its whole being as if to say, 'I'm here, alive and well,' something inexplicable welled up inside Izumi, and tears ran down his cheeks. He sobbed aloud, weeping without shame in front of their doctor and the nurses.

Whether the feeling that moved him was paternal instinct, he couldn't tell. But at that moment, he felt he'd finally found something inside he could rely on.

If he carried on with his life, trusting in whatever that something was, then one day he might find he'd become a parent. Just as his mother had surely done.

The sound of applause jolted Izumi back to the present.

Yuriko rose slowly, her performance completed.

As she turned, her eyes met Izumi's. For the first time in a long while, he saw in those eyes the mother he knew. 'Mum,' he breathed. Yuriko's lips moved, and he thought she called his name.

But the sound was lost in the thunder of applause.

The sun sank below the horizon, dyeing the sea the colour of ripe grapes.

Eyes fixed on that purple hue, Izumi called Kaori from the platform.

'How did it go?' she asked.

'Mum played really well. "Träumerei."'

'She's amazing, isn't she?'

'Yeah. A true pianist.'

'Izumi, what do you want to do about dinner?'

'I'll be pretty late, but I'd like to eat at home.'

'I made *nikujaga*. How about that?'

'Sounds good. Do you want me to pick up anything on my way?'

'Maybe some tomatoes. And some milk too.'

'Got it. I'll stop at the supermarket on my way home.'

'Oops. Hinata's crying. Sorry, I have to hang up.'

'No problem. I'll be home as soon as I can.'

On 27 August, a baby boy was born to Izumi and Kaori Kasai.

Weight: 3.47 kilograms. Name: Hinata. He was born three days past his due date.

15

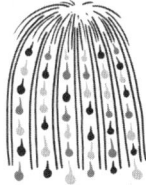

That smell comes from the garden of the house next door.

A sweet flower smell, like milk or fruit. A lovely smell. I stop in front of the garden to breathe it in and see a boy standing beside me. He's about the same age as me, I think. I feel like we've met somewhere before, but I can't remember where. 'Nice smell, isn't it?' the boy says, looking a little bashful. He must be shy. 'Uh-huh, a nice smell. What kind of flower is it?' I ask, and the boy points to small orange blossoms on a tree about my father's height. 'It's a fragrant olive tree. My mum told me.' 'Fragrant olive.' I repeat the name so that I won't forget. 'My mum likes the smell of fragrant olive.' 'Me too.' 'So you're just like my mum, then.' He smiles happily. I'm eating *omurice*. The boy sits across from me. There's a tulip on the table. The petals haven't opened yet. This must be the boy's house. But it seems so familiar. 'Where are your parents?' 'Mum's at work. I don't have a dad.' The tulip opens abruptly, then withers, petals dropping onto the table. Now there's a sunflower. It also blooms and withers swiftly. Time seems to pass quickly in this house. 'I like hayashi rice but I also like yellow foods,' the boy says, shovelling a spoonful of *omurice* into his mouth. 'Yellow foods?' 'Things like rolled omelette, banana, corn soup, sweet potato, castella cake, and the stuff inside cream puffs.' 'I like custard too.' 'That's what I thought. You're just like my mum. You, Mum and me, we all like the same things, so I think we could live together.' 'But I have to go.' 'Where to?' 'Home.' 'Where's that?' I don't know how to answer that question. Where's my home? I can't seem to remember now. Trying to remember how to remember, I run out of his house. A straight road stretches on forever in front of me. I walk down that road. There are no cars or motorcycles; no people either. No sounds or smells. I keep on walking and come to a huge whale sleeping in the middle of the road. His round tummy moves slowly up and down. 'Are you going?' The little boy is sitting on the back of the whale. 'Let's live together,' he calls. I want to stay and live with him, but I know that's not possible. Because this is a dream being dreamed by me, a newborn baby. A long, long dream, as long as someone's lifetime. Like a bursting bubble, I wake from the dream and find myself in a baby bed. I can't remember the dream I just had. I don't even know if I was dreaming. The boy looks at me sadly. 'Is this goodbye?' he asks. 'Maybe,' I say. 'Or maybe we'll meet in the future. But I love you.'

✳ ✳ ✳

Where does all this dust come from?

A thin layer of dust covered everything: photo frames, the rice cooker, paperbacks, vases, the grand piano.

Moving from the kitchen to the living room, from the bedroom to the front door, Izumi dusted and wiped and placed things in cardboard boxes. Countless music scores on the bookshelves. Mozart, Chopin, Bach, Beethoven, Schumann, Ravel, Satie. Countless melodies his mother had continued to play. They ran through Izumi's head to the sound of her piano.

Souvenir photos, ticket stubs from movies and concerts she and Izumi had enjoyed together, a little crockery *kamameshi* bento pot from a trip, the wristwatch he'd given her, mugs, a necklace. With their owner gone, everything looked faded. Or perhaps it was only in his memory that they'd appeared vibrant.

During her final days at Nagisa Home, Yuriko had slept all the time. From morning until noon, from noon until night. Had she spent all that time dreaming? Just as time and space in dreams become blurred, perhaps she'd eliminated the boundary between reality and everything else.

'Happy New Year.'

'Happy Birthday.'

Six days after they celebrated her birthday on New Year's Day, his mother had died of pneumonia as if drifting off to sleep. Even after the birth of his son, Izumi had spent New Year's Day with his mother. This was one of the few promises the two of them had made.

After an hour in the oven at the crematorium, Yuriko emerged as shards of pure white bone. The fragments of skeleton Izumi picked up with long bamboo chopsticks rattled drily as he placed them in an urn. The porcelain urn containing all that was left of his mother was lighter than he'd expected. Its lightness seemed to confirm that people are more than just their physical body. From the time of her death until the funeral was over, Izumi hadn't shed a single tear. It was going to take him a while to accept a world that lacked his mother.

Now, half a year later, Izumi was at his mother's house, which finally had a buyer. He'd set the ancient air conditioner to its strongest setting and spent two full days cleaning out the place, immersed all the while in the din of the cicadas. He discarded everything except a few usable items that could be donated to Nagisa Home. Almost a year had passed since Hinata's birth. Their apartment had filled rapidly with baby things – toys, clothes, dishes, a pram, leaving no room to keep anything from Yuriko's house. He felt some regret, but when he saw every available space buried in things for his son, he knew it was the right thing to do.

Izumi lay on the floor of Yuriko's empty house gazing at the windows of the apartment block beyond the garden. As he looked absently at the squares of light, the fatigue accumulated during the day's work washed over him, and he dozed off.

He was woken by a barrage of ear-splitting sounds.

Unsure if he was awake or still dreaming, he rose to his feet and saw fireworks bursting white against the dark blue sky.

'I always dreamed of someday living in a house where I could see fireworks.'

He thought he heard Yuriko's familiar voice beside him.

'By coincidence, my dream has come true.'

A few months after she returned from Kobe, his mother had decided to teach piano again in a different place. Izumi knew she was trying to start over as his mother by starting a new life, but he wasn't yet able to accept her renewed effort without reservations.

On the evening of the day they moved, they had sat side by side eating watermelon on the narrow porch under the eaves of their still empty house. Suddenly, fireworks had shot into the sky some distance away, part of an annual festival put on by the local government to mark the end of summer.

The burst was blocked by the tall apartment building beyond the garden, so that just the top half showed. Smaller bursts that exploded closer to the ground were merely sounds. Only the occasional big bursts, cut in half by the apartment block, appeared above the top.

'How pretty . . . They're the prettiest I've ever seen.' Yuriko smiled as she watched the semicircular explosions of light.

'But we can only see half.' Taking another bite of watermelon, Izumi stretched and craned his neck to see the fireworks more clearly.

'Yes, but to me, they're the most beautiful of all. It makes me so happy that today, in this empty house, the two of us saw fireworks. Even if we can only see half.'

Izumi thought they were beautiful too. And so was his mother, gazing up at them, her eyes moist.

'You know, I've always thought . . .' he said.

'What?'

'That fireworks are somehow sad. We forget them as soon as they're finished. We forget what colour they were, and what shape.'

'Maybe that's true . . . But even if you forget their colour or their shape, the memory of who you saw them with and how you felt at the time will stay with you.' His mother turned to look at Izumi and squeezed his hand. 'Right?'

'Yeah. I won't forget.' Gazing at the half fireworks, he murmured. 'I'm sure I'll remember today.'

'I wonder.' Yuriko looked at him and smiled. 'I bet you'll forget. We all forget things as we go along. But I think that's okay.'

Fireworks – white, red and yellow – burst one after the other above Izumi as he sat watching on his own.

Only half of each burst was visible. Gazing up at these 'half fireworks', which appeared before him now for the first time in about twenty years, he recalled in clear detail the conversation he'd had with his mother that day.

'I bet you'll forget.'

His mother's prediction resounded in his ears.

She'd remembered this whole time. He was the one who'd forgotten. He hadn't been able to show her one last time the fireworks she really wanted to see even though they were practically in her backyard.

A lump of sorrow and regret surged in his chest, shaking him to the core. Sinking to his knees, he curled up in a ball, unable to utter a word. All he could do was groan. Each semicircular burst brought back memories of his mother. Instead of words, tears poured from him, sliding down his cheeks.

Mum, I'm sorry. I completely forgot.

I forgot how you wept as you hugged me tight when I got lost at the amusement park. How you stayed up all night after work to sew my gym bag for school. How you always gave me half your share of the sweet rolled omelette. How you searched frantically for the flowered pouch I gave you for your birthday. How you cheered louder than anyone else at school sports' days, even though you felt uncomfortable being there on your own. I finally remember these things, Mum. I wish I'd thanked you before you forgot them. Things like how we celebrated, just the two of us, at a nearby restaurant after my graduation ceremony. Your sweat-stained back when you took me by bicycle to see a baseball game. The piping-hot sweet bean soup we ate together inside the snow hut. The electric guitar you bought me as a surprise; even though I actually wanted a different brand, it still made me happy. The trip we took together and the big fish I caught. That was the first time you'd ever fished too, wasn't it?

These things made me so happy. How could I have forgotten them?

'You'll start your new junior high tomorrow. Will you be all right?'

The doorbell had rung in the middle of the fireworks. Their luggage had arrived. The empty room quickly filled with cardboard boxes.

'Of course. I'm not a kid anymore.'

Izumi opened the boxes, removing only the things he would need the next day. His uniform, shoes, school bag, textbooks.

'Don't you mind using the uniform from your old school? You've worn it since you first entered junior high. I can buy you a new one.'

'It's okay, Mum. But there is one thing you could do for me.'

Izumi spread out the trousers and showed her a large hole in the knee.

'I tore it pretty badly. Could you sew it up for me?'

'Wow. That's impressive. How'd that happen?'

She took the trousers from him and traced the tear in the cloth with her finger.

'My friends and I were pretending to be pro wrestlers as a kind of sendoff, and I ripped the knee.'

'Seriously?' Yuriko chuckled, putting her hand to her mouth. 'I'm not sure I can fix it. The hole's too big, and the cloth around it is badly torn.'

'It doesn't matter, Mum. I'm fine with these trousers even if they're ripped and covered in holes.'

Half fireworks rose into the sky one after the other. Like the hundreds of flowers that had bloomed in the house where Izumi and Yuriko lived, they faded away, leaving behind only the memory of their beauty.

A breeze from the sea carried smoke and the scent of gunpowder.

The vivid half circles shining within Izumi's tear-blurred vision kept calling up images of his mother.

MEMORIES LOST BY A MOTHER AND RETRIEVED BY HER SON: AN AFTERWORD

by Kyoko Nakajima, novelist.

'So what makes us human is our memories, not our bodies?'

A minor character poses this question to an expert on artificial intelligence.

'That's right,' the expert responds.

Novels dealing with artificial intelligence inevitably touch upon this theme to some extent. Kazuo Ishiguro's *Klara and the Sun* does, as does the ambitious work *Transparence* by the acclaimed French novelist Marc Dugain. If memories make us who we are, what if they were transplanted into an imperishable body?

But at what point in life would a person's memories actually constitute their identity? Our memories change from day to day. For starters, we forget them or add things to them, and they also get jumbled up with dreams, stories and other people's memories.

Thankfully(!), the theme of *One Hundred Flowers* is not artificial intelligence.

It's the story of a son and his ageing mother who is losing her memory.

There are no science fiction elements in it whatsoever. Although the story is interwoven with the protagonist's recollections and the fragmented thoughts running through his mother's confused, Alzheimer's-impacted mind, the book stays within the bounds of realism. As I was reading, it struck me that dementia is a very human disease. Will the day come when artificial intelligence mimics the way we lose memory as well? Or will memory loss be considered an unnecessary function and thus never built in, even if AI is equipped to efficiently organise memories?

The protagonist, Izumi Kasai, is a thirty-seven-year-old man who works for a record company. His mother, Yuriko, raised him on her own. Izumi married a colleague from the same company and their first child will soon be born. The story is told dispassionately. The deterioration of Yuriko's memory; the trepidation with which Izumi and his wife, Kaori, face impending parenthood; the fairly stressful situations Izumi faces in his middle management position at work: these and other details unfold alongside recollections from Izumi's childhood. Penned with a quiet touch, these descriptions of the daily life of a relatable man underpin the novel's realism.

For many, the reality of elder care is this: filial duty calls when adult children are in the prime of their lives, busy with work and raising their own kids. While the stage of life at which each person begins caring for an elderly parent will of course differ, few are free of other obligations when the time comes. This is why most people tackle caregiving while struggling with the chronic guilt of not being able to do enough for their parents.

It's therefore easy to relate to Izumi in the first half of the book, when he's too overwhelmed with work to visit his mother and leaves her care to a helper as her symptoms grow worse. It's just as Yuriko's doctor says: 'At times, [dementia] seems to progress incredibly fast, only to abruptly slow down.' Families of dementia patients can't help but feel disorientated. Many readers will also see themselves in Izumi when, despite this fact, he resolves to do his best to support his mother as her condition deteriorates. Although he frequently loses patience with the things his increasingly forgetful mother does, he goes to her home after work and stays the night. When she's incontinent, he gives her a shower. When he hears she's wandered off, he rushes out to find her. That's the reality of elder care – it's tough.

Izumi comes across as an ordinary guy who cares about his mother. And, in fact, he is. There's no fixed formula for 'ordinary'; everyone has their own personality and every parent–child relationship is different. But there are certain scenes that make the reader think Izumi and his mother are unusually close. Take the scene at the beginning of the book, where mother and son spend New Year's together, just the two of them. On New Year's

Eve, Izumi goes to his mother's house where she lives alone; they welcome in the New Year by watching the New Year's Eve singing contest, *Kōhaku Uta Gassen*, on TV. New Year's Day is his mother's birthday, and spending it together seems to be their annual custom, one that started years before his mother got dementia. That Izumi would choose to leave his pregnant wife on her own and spend New Year's with his mother surely indicates an exceptional closeness.

Take also the scene where Izumi recalls how his mother burst into tears when he told her he was getting married. 'Up until now I had to focus all my energy on surviving,' she says. 'I thought that . . . I'd finally be able to do all the things parents usually do with their children.' While many mothers may inwardly feel dismayed when they hear their son is getting married, the reaction of this single mother, the piano teacher portrayed as a dependable parent, somehow comes across as a little odd, in a way that stands apart from the confusion she exhibits as someone with Alzheimer's.

Apparently, wandering is a peripheral symptom, not a core feature of dementia. Rather than automatically beginning with the onset of the condition, it occurs in response to some stimulus after dementia has impaired cognitive functioning. This is why some people with dementia wander while others don't. Despite this, however, wandering is generally equated with dementia, when really the focus should be on what inspires that behaviour.

Yuriko wanders off several times. It becomes clear as the story progresses that this behaviour is connected to a place deep inside her. From the very beginning, she has been searching for her lost son. As a boy, Izumi frequently got lost, and Yuriko had to find him. When Izumi begins searching for his mother, he dredges up memories of his childhood. Why, he wonders, did he keep getting lost? And what, then, is causing his ageing mother's behaviour?

At the heart of this novel is the memory of a decisive year in the lives of this mother and son, a memory they have both worked hard to erase. While Izumi's mother is already letting it go, or befuddling it with other memories, the things they had sealed away are thrust upon Izumi. This confrontation with the past comes in the form of a vivid memoir his mother wrote during that year, a diary he stumbles across in her house after she enters a nursing home.

The reader becomes aware that Yuriko and Izumi's relationship is very peculiar because of that year. The special nature of this parent and child, their odd closeness and their somewhat ambivalent distance, is starkly revealed.

The book's charm is the wonderful balance the author's portrayal strikes between a mother losing her memory and a son regaining his. People in the busy prime of their lives rarely have time to recall childhood memories. But the thought of losing one's parent can trigger a flood of things shoved away, deep within the recesses of the mind. 'I bet you'll forget.' Izumi remembers his mother telling him this. He remembers what it was he'd forgotten when she forgets it herself.

Dementia is often portrayed as a cruel disease that suddenly erases a person's humanity. As if those with dementia forget who they are and those they love, lose their personality, and are no longer human. Yet I doubt that's how it works. This novel, I believe, captures this point perfectly. People lose their memory. But within that process, the individual continues to be themselves to a painful, heartbreaking and endearing degree. Izumi's mother, Yuriko, becomes defenceless, exposed. She is Yuriko the child, Yuriko the young mother, Yuriko the woman who dreamed of living just for herself, and Yuriko who chose to return to her son. Her dementia is indeed a process of giving up her memories, but like sparks from Japanese sparklers, the varied faces Yuriko revealed during her final year of life ignite many memories for Izumi. In that sense, for those engaged in their care, an elderly dementia patient's existence is in no way meaningless or empty.

Someday, Izumi will probably forget too. He will lose even those memories he regained. Maybe memories are something that cannot be passed on to anyone. But Izumi will surely share something of them with his son. Even if he never tells his son directly about Yuriko, something new will be born and spoken of between father and son, and in exchange for letting his own memories go, Izumi may inspire his son to remember.

Some say it's our memories that make us human.

Even after finishing this book, I remained enveloped in its warmth.